She was inviting h[...] Christmas dinner [...] family.

Part of him was totally enraptured by the idea. But it terrified him far more.

What did he know about family Christmases? He could remember just one happy Christmas from his childhood: the year he had spent with his grandparents.

"Forget it. I should never have invited you." She turned away.

"It's silly," she went on. "You don't have to feel obligated. Just pretend I never opened my big, stupid mouth."

The big, stupid mouth he couldn't stop thinking about? The one that haunted his dreams, that he could still taste every time he closed his eyes?

"Jenna—"

"Just forget it," she said. "It was a crazy impulse."

"No, it wasn't. It was very sweet."

Her gaze flashed to his and he lost the battle for control. He stepped forward, pulled her against him and kissed her, just as he had dreamed about doing....

Dear Reader,

I love everything about Christmas, from the music to the decorating to the shopping! It's particularly joyful to share the holiday with children, and mine especially love spending time in the kitchen with me. This is one of our favorite recipes—my youngest thinks it's very cool to help me roll the dough balls in the cinnamon-sugar mix! I hope he never grows out of it.

SNICKERDOODLES

Ingredients:

1 cup butter, softened
1 cup shortening (I use margarine, softened)
3 cups white sugar
4 eggs
4 teaspoons vanilla extract
5 1/2 cups all-purpose flour
4 teaspoons cream of tartar
2 teaspoons baking powder
1/2 teaspoon salt
1/2 cup white sugar
2-3 teaspoons ground cinnamon, to taste

Directions:

1. Preheat oven to 400°F (200°C)
2. Cream together butter, shortening or margarine, 3 cups sugar, eggs and vanilla with electric hand mixer or in food processor.
3. Blend in flour, cream of tartar, baking soda and salt.
4. Shape dough by rounded spoonfuls into balls.
5. Mix 1/2 cup sugar and cinnamon. Roll dough balls in mixture to coat.
6. Place 2 inches apart on ungreased or parchment-lined baking sheets. Bake 8-10 minutes until just firm. Don't overcook.
7. Remove immediately from baking sheets and enjoy!

May your holidays be joyful and filled with love.

RaeAnne Thayne

THE COWBOY'S CHRISTMAS MIRACLE

RAEANNE THAYNE

SPECIAL EDITION

Published by Silhouette Books

America's Publisher of Contemporary Romance

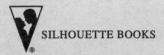 SILHOUETTE BOOKS

ISBN-13: 978-0-373-24933-6
ISBN-10:   0-373-24933-0

THE COWBOY'S CHRISTMAS MIRACLE

Copyright © 2008 by RaeAnne Thayne

This edition published by arrangement with Harlequin Books S.A.

Visit Silhouette Books at www.eHarlequin.com

Printed in U.S.A.

Books by RaeAnne Thayne

Silhouette Special Edition

Silhouette Romantic Suspense

*Outlaw Hartes
†The Searchers
**The Women of Brambleberry House
††The Cowboys of Cold Creek
§The Wilder Family

RAEANNE THAYNE

finds inspiration in the beautiful northern Utah mountains, where she lives with her husband and three children. Her books have won numerous honors, including a RITA® Award nomination from Romance Writers of America and a Career Achievement Award from *Romantic Times BOOKreviews* magazine. RaeAnne loves to hear from readers and can be reached through her Web site at www.raeannethayne.com.

Chapter One

The brats were at it again.

Carson McRaven scowled as he drove under the massive, ornately carved log arch to the Raven's Nest Ranch.

He owned five thousand acres of beautiful eastern Idaho ranch land. A reasonable person might suppose that with that kind of real estate, he had a good chance of escaping Jenna Wheeler and her hell spawn.

Instead, it seemed like every time he turned around, some little towheaded imp was invading his space—sledding down his private driveway, bothering his horses, throwing snowballs at his ranch sign.

A month ago—the last time he had found time to come out to his new ranch from San Francisco—he had caught them trying to jump their swaybacked little paint ponies over his new electric fence. The time before, he had found them building a tree house in one of the trees on *his* property. And in September, he had ended up with a broken window in the gleaming new horse barn and his foreman had found a baseball amid the shattered glass inside.

He couldn't seem to turn around without finding one or more of them wandering around his land. They were three annoying little flies in the ointment of what would otherwise be the perfect bucolic retreat from the hectic corporate jungle of San Francisco.

When he bought the property from Jenna Wheeler, he thought he had been fine with her stipulation that she retain one twenty-acre corner of land for her ranch. He was getting five thousand acres more, bordered by National Forest land. One little nibble out of the vast pie shouldn't bother him. But in the ten months since they closed on the deal, that little nibble sat in his craw like an unshelled walnut.

Every time he drove up Cold Creek Canyon to Raven's Nest and spotted her two-story frame house in the corner of his land, he ground his back teeth and wished to hell he had fought harder to buy the whole property so he could have torn it down to have this entire area to himself.

And to make matters even more aggravating, apparently the Wheeler urchins didn't understand the concept of trespassing. Yes, their mother had paid for the broken window and had made them take the tree house down, plank by plank. After her frustrated reaction when he told her about their steeplechase through his pasture, he would have expected her to put the fear of God into them.

Or at least the fear of their mother.

But here one of them was balancing on the snow-covered split-rail fence that lined his driveway, arms outstretched like he was a miniature performer on a circus high wire, disaster just a heartbeat away while his brothers watched from the sidelines.

Carson slowed the SUV he kept stored at the Jackson Hole airport, an hour away, though he hesitated to hit the brakes just yet.

He ought to just let the kids fall where they may. What was a broken arm or two to him? If the Wheeler hellions wanted to be little daredevils, what business was it of his? He could just turn the other way and keep on driving up to the house. He had things to do, calls to make, fresh Idaho air to breathe.

On the other hand, the boys were using *his* fence as their playground. If one of them took a tumble and was seriously injured, he could just hear their mother accusing him of negligence or even tacit complicity because he didn't try to stop them when he had the chance.

He sighed. He couldn't ignore them and just keep on driving, as much as he might desperately want to. He braked to a stop and rolled down the window to the cold December air. "Hey kid, come down from there before somebody gets hurt."

He was grimly aware he was only a sidestep away from sounding like a grumpy old man yelling at the neighbor's kids to stay the hell off his grass.

The boys apparently hadn't heard the rumble of his engine. They blinked and he could see surprise in all their expressions. The younger two looked apprehensive but the biggest boy jutted out his chin.

"We do it all the time," he boasted. "Kip's the best. Show him."

"Maybe we should go home." The medium-sized one with the wire-rim glasses slanted a nervous look toward Carson. "Remember, Mom told us this morning to come home right from the bus stop to do chores."

"That's a good idea," Carson encouraged. "Go on home, now."

"Don't be such a scaredy-cat," the older one taunted, then turned to the other boy, who was watching their interaction closely, as if trying to predict who the victor would be. "It's okay, Kip. Show him."

Before Carson could figure out a way to climb out of his truck and yank the kid off the fence, the boy took another step forward and then another.

He grinned at Carson. "See? I can go super far without falling!" he exclaimed. "One time I went from the gate all the way to that big pine tree."

The words were barely out of his mouth when his boot hit an icy patch of railing.

His foot slid to the edge though not completely off the log, but his arms wheeled desperately as he tried to keep his balance. It was a losing battle, apparently. His feet went flying off the fence first and the rest of him followed. Even from here, above the sound of his vehicle's engine, Carson could hear the thud of the boy's head bumping the log rail on the way down.

Damn it.

He shut off the vehicle and jumped out, hurrying to where the boy lay still in the snow. The middle boy was already crouched in the snow next to him, but his attention was focused more on his older brother than the injured younger one.

"You're such a dope, Hayden." He glared. "Why'd you make him do it? Mom's gonna kill us both now!"

"I didn't make him! He didn't have to do it just because I told him to. He's got a brain, doesn't he?"

"More of one than you do," the middle boy snapped.

Carson decided it was past time for him to step in and focus attention on the important thing, their dazed brother, who looked as if he'd had the wind and everything else knocked out of his sails.

"Come on, kid. Talk to me."

The boy met his gaze, his green eyes wide and a little unfocused. After a few seconds, he drew in a deep breath and then he started to wail, softly at first and then loud enough to spook up a couple of magpies that had come to see what the commotion was about.

"Come on, Kip. You're okay," the middle kid soothed, patting him on the shoulder, which only seemed to make the kid howl louder.

What Carson knew about bawling kids would fit inside the cap of a ballpoint pen. His instincts were telling him to hop right back into his SUV and leave the boys to fend for themselves. Knowing how rowdy and reckless they were, this couldn't be the first time one of them had taken a tumble.

But he couldn't do it. Not with the kid looking at him out of those drippy eyes and the other two watching him with such contrasting expressions—one hostile and the other obviously expecting him to take charge.

The boy swiped at his tears with the sleeve of his parka and scrambled to sit up in the snow. Carson watched his efforts to make sure he wasn't favoring any stray limbs, but nothing appeared to be damaged beyond repair.

He would let their mother deal with it all, he decided. It would serve her right for letting them run wild. "Come on. I'll give you all a ride back to your house."

The middle boy eyed him warily. "We're not supposed to get in strangers' cars."

"He's not a stranger," the older boy snapped with a return to that belligerence. "He's Mr. McRaven, the dude who stole our ranch."

"I didn't—" Instinctively, Carson started to defend himself, then broke off the words. How ridiculous, that he would feel compelled to offer any explanations at all to a trio of rowdy little hellions.

"You want me to drive your little brother home or would you like to carry him all the way yourselves?" he asked.

The older boys exchanged a glance and then Hayden, the older one, shrugged. "Whatever."

He personally would have preferred the latter option, especially after he scooped up the boy and carried him to the SUV, which resulted in even more tears. Again, he wished fiercely that he had just kept on driving when he'd seen them on his fence. If not for that ill-fated decision to stop, none of this would have happened and right now he would be saddling up one of his horses for a good hard ride into the snowy mountains.

He set the boy in the backseat then turned back to the other boys. "You two coming?"

The middle boy with the glasses nodded and climbed in beside his brother but the older one looked as if he would rather be dragged behind the SUV than accept a ride from him. After a long moment, though, he shrugged and went around to the other door.

The only sound in the SUV as they drove the short distance up the driveway to the Wheeler house was the little one's steady sobs and a few furtive attempts to comfort him.

The two-story cedar farmhouse was charming in its own way, he supposed, with the shake roof and the old-fashioned swing on the wide front porch. But no one could possibly miss that a passel of children lived here. From the basketball hoop above the garage to the Santa Claus and reindeer figures in the yard to the sleds propped against the porch steps, everything shouted *family*.

It was completely alien to him, and all the more terrifying because of it.

For about half a second, he was tempted just to dump the lot of them there at their doorstep but he supposed that sort of callousness wouldn't exactly be considered neighborly around these parts.

Fighting his reluctance, he climbed out of the SUV and opened the rear door, then scooped out the still-crying Kip.

They all moved together up the porch steps but before Carson could knock at the door, Hayden burst through and shouted for his mother.

"Mom, Kip fell down off the fence by the bus stop. It was an accident. Nobody dared him or anything, he just went up by himself and slipped."

Warmth seeped out from the open doorway, along with the mingled aroma of cinnamon and sugar and pine.

The comforting, enticing scents of home.

The Wheeler boys might be wild, fatherless urchins with a distracted mother and more courage than sense. But Carson couldn't help the niggle of envy for what they had, things they no doubt would not even appreciate until much later in their lives.

"You can come inside," the middle boy said shyly. "Mom doesn't like us to leave the door open."

Feeling a bit encroaching for walking into her house, even at the permission of her kid, Carson took a few steps inside, just enough that he could close the door behind him.

He instantly wondered if he had accidentally stepped into one of those annoying Christmas shops in Jackson Hole. Every inch of the foyer seemed to be decorated with greenery or muted red gingham ribbons or ornaments of some sort. A wide staircase led upstairs and the banister was a wild riot of evergreen boughs and twinkling lights. A small trio of fir trees in the corner of the landing were decorated with homespun decorations from nature—pinecones, dried orange slices, even a couple of miniature bird nests.

Through the doorway into the living room, he caught a glimpse of a big evergreen tree, decorated with sloppy paper chains and a hodgepodge of decorations that seemed lopsided, even at a cursory glance.

He barely had time for the few observations to register when the boys' mother bustled into the foyer wearing a red-and-green pin-striped apron and carrying the littlest Wheeler—and the only girl of the bunch.

Jenna stopped dead when she saw him, her ethereal blond hair slipping free of its confines, as usual. "Oh! Mr. McRaven! This is a surprise. Hayden didn't mention you were here."

"I happened to be passing by in time to see the, uh, accident. I couldn't just leave him out there."

"Of course you couldn't," she said. Though her tone was polite enough, he was quite sure he caught a whiff of skepticism. He tried not to let it rankle.

"Thank you for your kindness in bringing them home. I'm very sorry they troubled you again."

Her tone was cooler than the icicles hanging off her porch. The Widow Wheeler didn't like him very much. She had made that fact abundantly clear over the last ten months since he purchased her property.

Oh, she was polite enough in their sporadic dealings, never

overtly rude. But he ran an international technology innovation company, which was a hell of a lot like a good poker game. Keen powers of observation were a vital job skill and he had developed his own to a fine degree. He couldn't miss the tiny shadow of disdain in her green eyes when she talked to him.

"Where would you like me to set your little injured buckaroo here?"

"I'll take him."

She set the little one on the floor and the girl toddled to a wicker basket full of toys in the living room and proceeded to start yanking the contents out, one by one, and tossing them on the floor.

Jenna stepped closer to Carson and reached for the boy in his arms, whose wails had trickled to the occasional sniffle. Carson's leather coat was open and as she took the child from him, her hands brushed against his chest for only an instant.

Even through his cotton shirt, he could feel the warmth of her hands, the small, delicate flutter of them and his stomach muscles tightened.

It was a ridiculous reaction, one that first stunned, then exasperated him. He really needed to expend a little more energy on his social life if he could be attracted to Jenna Wheeler, even on an instinctively physical level.

Sure, she was soft and pretty, with that wispy honey-blond hair and her undeniable curves and those big green eyes all her children had inherited.

But she had that unfortunate baggage shackled around her neck. Four wild kids, the youngest just a toddler.

Apparently, the only thing the injured one of her children needed was his mother. She sat down on a nearby wooden rocking chair. The boy snuggled against her chest and she pressed a kiss on his forehead.

"Hush now, sweetheart. Where does it hurt?"

He sniffled a little and pointed to the back of his head that had conked against the railing. "I hurt my head."

"I'm so sorry." She kissed the spot he showed her, her eyes tender and maternal, and Carson's stomach muscles tightened again, this time with a weird, indefinable *something* he couldn't have explained.

"Better?" she asked.

"A little," the boy answered.

"Jolie and I made your favorite snickerdoodles this afternoon, didn't we, ladybug?" she smiled at the little girl, who beamed back in the middle of pulling the ornaments off the tree. "They're for the party tomorrow but when you feel better, you can go into the kitchen and get one."

Cookies were apparently the magic remedy. Who knew? The boy's sniffles dried up and after only twenty seconds more, he slid off his mother's lap.

"I feel a lot better now," he announced. "Can I have a cookie now?"

"Yes. Grab one each for your brothers."

He flashed his mother a smile and raced from the room at top speed, leaving Carson alone with the two equally terrifying Wheeler females.

"Thank you again for bringing him home. It's a long walk up the driveway for a kid with an owie."

"I guess I was lucky to be there at the right time," he said.

"He fell off a fence, you said?"

He hesitated, not sure quite how to answer her. She knew his feelings about the boys trespassing on his property and he was suddenly reluctant to dredge all that up. On the other hand, she needed to know what they had been up to.

"The split-rail fence just past where our access roads fork."

"On the Raven's Nest side," she surmised correctly.

"Yeah."

"What was he doing on a fence?" She looked as if she wasn't quite sure she wanted to hear his answer.

"Tightrope walking, apparently."

She let out a long, frustrated sigh. "I have warned them and warned them to stay off your property. I hate that they've put me in this position again."

"What position would that be?"

"Having to apologize to you once more."

Again that sliver of disdain flickered in her eyes and he did his best not to bristle, though he was aware his voice was harder than he would have normally used.

"I certainly don't want to tell you how to be a parent, but you have to do something to get the point across a little more forcefully to them. A working ranch is a dangerous place for three young boys, ma'am."

Her expression turned even more glacial. "I believe I'm aware of just how dangerous a ranch can be, Mr. McRaven. Probably better than you."

He remembered too late just why she had been forced to sell her ranch to him. Her husband had been killed in a tragic accident on the ranch two years earlier, leaving behind bills and obligations Jenna Wheeler had been unable to take care of without selling the land that had been in her husband's family for generations.

He regretted his tactlessness but his point was still valid. "Then you, more than anybody, should stress those dangers to your boys. There are a hundred ways they could get hurt, as today's accident only reinforced."

"Thank you for your concern," she said with that tight, dismissive voice that seemed so discordant in contrast to her soft feminine features. "I'll be sure to tell them once again to stay away from Raven's Nest."

"Do that."

He shoved on his Stetson, knowing he sounded like a first-class jerk, but he didn't know how else to get the message across to her or her boys except with bluntness. "I know neither of us wants any of your boys to be seriously hurt. But I have to tell you, I refuse to be held responsible if they are, especially when you've been warned again and again about their trespassing habits."

"Warning duly noted, Mr. McRaven."

He sighed in frustration. He successfully negotiated corporate deals all the time, had built McRaven Enterprises into an international force to be reckoned with in only a dozen years. So why couldn't he seem to have any interaction with this woman that didn't end with him feeling he was a cross between Simon Legree and Lord Voldemort?

He needed to have his people make her another offer for this land and the house, he decided. As far as he was concerned, the only way to solve their particular quandary would be for her to sell him this section and move her little family somewhere she could be someone else's problem.

She closed the door behind Carson McRaven, wondering how it was possible for a man to be so very physically attractive—with that dark, wavy hair and eyes of such a deep blue she couldn't help staring every time she saw them—yet have all the personality appeal of a wolverine with a sore snout.

The sale of the ranch had mostly been carried out through third parties. Jenna had known he was some kind of a Bay Area financial wizard and she had met him briefly when he had come to inspect the Wagon Wheel, as it all used to be called. Sure, he had been brisk and businesslike. But she had admired his plans to experiment with more environmentally sound ranching practices and he had seemed decent enough in that short meeting.

Of course, that was before her boys apparently decided to make it their personal mission to be as mischievous as possible—and to do it on Carson McRaven's property.

She couldn't blame him for being frustrated. She was at her wit's end trying to keep them on their side of the property line. But she resented his unspoken implication that her boys were feral banshees allowed to run wild through the mountains.

"Mom, do I still have to do chores?" Kip asked in a plaintive kind of voice. "Hayden says I do."

"I think this once, maybe Hayden can take out the garbage for you, if we ask him nicely."

"My head still hurts."

She pulled him toward her and gave him another kiss, just for good measure. "I don't think it's broken. Bruised a little, maybe, but you've got a pretty tough nut."

"It was scary when I fell."

"You shouldn't have been up on Mr. McRaven's fence, right? I don't want you boys up there again. Next time you might hurt yourself even worse. What if you fell inside the pasture when one of those bulls of his were close by?"

"But I'm really good at it. I like being good at something. Hayden's good at riding the ponies and Drew is good at math and stuff. But I can't do anything."

"You're only six years old, bud. You'll figure out what you're good at soon enough."

"Mom!" Hayden called out. "Can we eat these tart thingies in here?"

"No," she answered as she picked up Jolie and headed back toward the kitchen. "They're for the party tomorrow."

"Everything you make is for some party or a reception or something stupid like that. Why can't we eat any of it?" Hayden complained.

"You can have another snickerdoodle after you feed the horses. I made plenty of those."

"I wanted a tart," her oldest muttered.

Naturally. If she had told him the snickerdoodles were off-limits, that would have been the only thing he wanted. She loved him dearly but this sudden contrariness of his sometimes drove her crazy. Hayden was only ten and she already felt like she was battling all the teen stuff her friends had warned her to expect.

Maybe there was a lesson in that for her, she thought after she had shooed Hayden and Drew out the door to take care of their chores in the barn and returned to preparing for her last holiday party of the season.

Carson McRaven was definitely off-limits to her. Beyond the fact that she disliked him personally, he was a multimillionaire tech investor with a reputation for finding products the world didn't realize it couldn't do without, while she was an overtired widow with a struggling catering business and more obligations than she could begin to handle.

She wasn't genuinely interested in any man. In the first place, when on earth would she have the time for one? Between helping the boys with homework, taking care of Jolie, the upkeep on their remaining twenty acres, taking care of her mother-in-law and starting up a struggling catering business, she had nothing left.

In the second, her heart still ached for Joe and probably always would. After two years alone, she still woke up in the middle of the night sometimes and turned over, trying to snuggle into his warmth, only to find a cold void where he used to be. Just like the one inside her heart.

She pushed away the echo of pain out of long practice as she rolled more cookie-dough balls in the cinnamon sugar mix, then set them on the cookie sheet.

Yes, every time she saw Carson McRaven, her heart seemed to race a bit faster and her stomach trembled. She didn't like her reaction but it was a little easier to comprehend when she told herself it was only because he represented the unattainable.

She almost believed it, too.

Chapter Two

She was impossibly stuck.

Jenna revved the engine one more time and tried to rock her van out of the deep snowbank just outside the turnoff for the Wagon Wheel. Carson McRaven might call it Raven's Nest now but to her this would always be the Wagon Wheel, named after three generations of Wheelers who had worked this corner of eastern Idaho in the western shadow of the Grand Tetons.

She glared at the clock on her dashboard and then at the snow still falling hard outside the van windows. Of all the miserable, rotten, lousy times to be stuck. She had a van full of food and an extremely short window of time in which to prepare it.

She thought she had everything so carefully orchestrated in order to have all the last-minute details ready for the party she was catering that evening. The moment the boys climbed onto the school bus, she had loaded Jolie into her van and driven to Idaho Falls, where the grocery selection was more extensive—and fresher—than anything she could find here in Pine Gulch.

She had budgeted a little over two hours, figuring that would give her time to drive there, shop and then drive home.

Naturally, it started snowing the minute she left Idaho Falls and hadn't let up the entire forty-five-minute drive since then. At least four inches had fallen, laying a slick layer of white over everything.

As frustrating as she found the snow to drive in, it did set the perfect scene for Christmas. The evergreen trees on the mountainside looked as if they had been drizzled with Royal Icing and Cold Creek matched its name by burbling through patches of ice.

She only wished she had time to enjoy it all. Then again, if she had taken a few extra minutes to slow down and pay attention to her driving instead of her extensive to-do list, she wouldn't be in this predicament. Instead, she had been driving just a hair too fast when she headed over the bridge just before the driveway split, one route going toward Carson McRaven's new, huge log house and the other heading toward home.

Just as she made the turn, her van tires slid and she hadn't been able to pull out of the skid in time before landing in the drift.

She knew better than this. That was the most aggravating thing about the whole situation. She had been driving these Idaho winter roads since she was fourteen years old. She knew the importance of picking a driving speed appropriate for conditions, knew that this section could be slick, knew she had to stay focused on the road—not on the baby field-green salad she still had to make or the tricky vodka blush sauce she still hadn't perfected for the penne.

But she had just been in such a big darn hurry to make everything just right for this party. It was her biggest event yet, and the one she hoped would make her the go-to person for catering in this area.

None of which would happen if she didn't manage to extricate herself from this blasted snowdrift.

She shoved the van into Reverse again. If she could just get a little traction, the front-wheel drive on her van might be able to do the job. But try as she might, shifting between Reverse and Drive to try rocking out of the snow, the wheels just spun, kicking up snow and mud and gravel behind her.

Blast it all. She wanted to cry at the delay but she just didn't have the time.

She looked in the rearview mirror to the backseat, where Jolie was babbling quietly to herself in her car seat and playing with her favorite stuffed dog, bouncing him on her lap then twirling him in dizzying circles.

"Well, bug, it looks like we're walking home. We'll go get your daddy's big, bad pickup truck with the four-wheel drive and come back for the food."

No big deal, she assured herself. She only had to walk a quarter mile from here down the driveway to the house. If she hurried, she could make it in ten minutes and be back here in fifteen.

She pulled Jolie out of her car seat. Her daughter beamed at her. "Walk, Mommy?"

"Looks like."

She settled her daughter on her hip, grateful she had at least had the foresight to wear her boots that morning, even though it hadn't been snowing when she left home.

She had just crossed her slide tracks and started up her long driveway that followed the river when she heard a pickup truck coming down the hill from Raven's Nest.

She only had time to whisper a prayer that it would be Neil or Melina Parker, McRaven's ranch foreman and his wife who served as caretaker when Carson wasn't there, before the pickup pulled up next to her.

Apparently nobody was listening to her prayers today. She sighed as Carson rolled down the passenger-side window.

"You look like you could use a hand."

Her pulse did that stupid little jumpy thing at his deep voice and she could feel her face heat up. She could only hope he didn't notice, probably too busy thinking what an idiot she was for driving into a snowbank like that.

"I was just planning to walk to my house for my pickup. I've got groceries in the back I need to take care of quickly."

"Put your baby back in the van, where it's warm and out of the snow. I should have a tow rope in the pickup truck somewhere. I'll have you out in a second."

She wanted to balk at his commanding tone and tell him to go to Hades but for the first time in her life she understood the old saying about pride being a luxury she simply couldn't afford right now.

She should just be grateful for his help, she reminded herself, even if she found it both humiliating and annoying to be obligated to him once more.

"I'm sorry to trouble you. That's two days in a row now that you've had to come to our rescue."

He made a kind of rueful grimace that plainly told her he wasn't any more thrilled than she was about the situation, while he fished around behind the seat of the pickup and pulled out a thick braided red tow rope. "Here we go."

Before she quite knew how it happened, he was crouched in the snow, attaching the tow to her rear bumper. McRaven probably had more money in loose change than she would see in any lifetime but he didn't seem to have any qualms about dirtying his hands a little. It was an unexpected facet of a man who she was beginning to believe just may be more complicated than she might have guessed. He hitched the other end of the tow around his own pickup's bumper, then came to her window again.

"Okay, now start it up and just steer out when you feel your van pull free of the snowbank. You should be on your way in a minute or two."

She nodded and waited while he climbed back into the truck. Over her shoulder, she watched him engage the four-wheel drive of his truck. He appeared to barely ease forward but just that tiny extra bit of help was enough to accomplish what ten minutes of spinning her tires in the ice and snow hadn't been able to do.

Another life lesson for her, maybe? she wondered ruefully. Accepting a little help in the short-term might be humiliating but could save much heartache and struggle.

She didn't have time to wax philosophical this morning, not when her to-do list felt longer than her driveway and just as slickly treacherous.

"Thank you," she said through her open window when Carson returned to her vehicle to unhook the tow rope.

"No problem. You're going to want to take things slow until that access road gets plowed. I slid about four times coming down the hill from my place."

"I know. I was just in too big of a hurry and wasn't paying attention to how fast I was going. I'll be sure to concentrate better now. Thanks again."

He studied her for a moment, then she saw his blue eyes shift to Jolie in the backseat, who beamed at him and waved.

"Hi, mister," she chirped, which was what she called every adult male of her acquaintance, from her Uncle Paul to the pastor at church to the bagger at the grocery store.

"Hi," he said, his voice a little more gruff than usual, then he stepped back and waved her on.

With her wipers on high, Jenna slowly put the van in gear and inched through the swirling snow that seemed to have increased dramatically in just the few moments since Carson arrived. She was so busy paying attention to the road—and trying to keep from sliding into the icy Cold Creek that paralleled her driveway—that she didn't notice the headlights behind her until she was nearly home.

What was Carson doing? She frowned as his pickup continued to tail her along the winding drive. Maybe something had fallen out of her van when she was stopped and he was returning it. Or maybe he decided she needed more of a lecture on her winter driving skills, or lack thereof.

She wouldn't put it past him. The man seemed to want to give her plenty of advice on child rearing. Judging by past comments, he apparently put her abilities as a mother somewhere between incompetent and negligible and seemed to think she let her boys run wild and free through the countryside with no supervision.

And now he probably thought she was just as inept at driving. She pulled into her garage and stepped out of her driver's seat to walk back outside, already squaring her shoulders for another confrontation.

"Is something wrong?" she asked coolly when he rolled down his window.

"I just wanted to make sure you made it home safely. I'll send one of my guys over with the tractor to plow the driveway in case you need to get out soon."

She blinked at him as hard, wind-whipped snowflakes stung her cheeks. Her first reaction was astonishment and a quick spurt of gratitude, both that he was concerned at her welfare enough to follow her home and that he would offer to help her plow her road.

One less chore to do, right? she thought. Especially since digging out the driveway wasn't among her favorites.

At the same time, she didn't want him to think she needed to be looked after like some kind of charity case.

"I have a tractor with a front plow," she answered. "I can take care of it. I would have done it earlier but it wasn't snowing when I left for Idaho Falls."

She regretted her words the moment she uttered them. She didn't owe Carson McRaven any explanations."

"I'll send someone," he answered. "Stay warm."

Before she could protest, he hit the button to automatically wind up his window, put his big pickup in gear and drove away.

She watched him go for a moment as the wind howled through the bare tops of the cottonwoods and lodgepole pine along the river. Her neighbor was nothing if not confounding. She couldn't quite peg him into a neat compartment. On the one hand, he was arrogant and supercilious and seemed to think her family's entire focus in life was to annoy him as much as humanly possible.

On the other, he *had* been kind to her boys the day before and he had certainly helped her just now when he really could have looked the other way.

She shivered as the wind cut through her parka and turned back to the garage. She had far more critical things to occupy her mind with right now than obsessing—again—about her new neighbor.

Jolie chattered away as Jenna carried her into the house. Only about one word in three was recognizable and none of them seemed to require a response, but her daughter never seemed to mind carrying on a conversation by herself.

She was a complete joy and far more easygoing than any of the boys had been. She didn't complain when Jenna took her straight from her car seat to her high chair and set some dry cereal and a sippy cup of milk on the tray while she went out to cart the groceries inside from the van.

Just as she was carrying the last armload in, the phone rang. She thought about ignoring it, but with three boys in school, she couldn't take the risk it might be one of their teachers or, heaven forbid, the school principal.

"Phone, Mama. Phone."

"I know, honey. I'll get it."

She quickly set down the bags on the last clear counter space in the kitchen and lunged for the cordless handset before the answering machine could pick up.

"Sorry. Hello," she said breathlessly.

"Hello, my dear."

Jenna smiled at the instantly recognizable voice on the other end of the line. Viviana Cruz was one of her favorite people on earth. She and her second husband had a ranch a little farther up the creek and raised beautiful Murray Gray cattle.

"Viviana! How are you?"

"*Bien, gracias*. And you? How do you do? Busy, busy, I would guess."

"You would be right, as usual, Viv. I'm running a little late, but I promise, all will be ready in time."

"I do not doubt this. Not for *un momentito*. The food will be delicious, I have no worries."

At least one of them was confident, Jenna thought as nerves fluttered in her stomach. This job was important to her, not only professionally but personally. Viviana had taken a big risk hiring her to cater the holiday event she was hosting for the local cattle growers' association, of which she served as president. This was the biggest job Jenna had undertaken since she started her catering business six months earlier. Before this, she had mostly done small parties, but this involved ranchers and business owners from this entire region of southeastern Idaho.

Viv had told her there would be people coming from the Jackson Hole area, as well. She planned to have her business cards out where everyone could see and made a mental note to also stick the magnetic banner on her van that read *Cold Creek Cuisine*.

"Thanks, Viv. I hope so."

"I was checking to see if you are needing any help."

Unfortunately, the answer to that was an unequivocal *yes* but she couldn't admit defeat yet. She could do this. She had planned everything carefully and much of the food was already prepped. Her sister-in-law and niece were coming over in a couple of hours to help her with last-minute things, so she should be all right.

"I think I'll be okay. Thanks for offering, though."

"You are bringing your children tonight, yes?"

Oh, heavens, what a nightmare *that* would be. "No. Not this time, Viv. My niece, Erin, is coming out to the house to tend to them while Terri helps me serve your guests."

"I so love those little darlings of yours."

She smiled as she put away the groceries, the handset tucked into her shoulder. Viv was one of the most genuine people Jenna knew. She was enormously blessed to have such wonderful neighbors. After the tractor accident that critically injured Joe, all the neighbors along the Cold Creek had rallied around her. Viv's husband Guillermo and the Daltons, who owned the biggest spread in the area, had all rushed to help her out.

While she had been numbly running between the ranch and the trauma center in Idaho Falls for those awful weeks Joe was in a coma, they had stepped in to care for her children, to bring in the fall alfalfa crop, to round up the Wagon Wheel cattle from the summer range.

She could never repay any of them.

"They adore you, too," she said now to Viv. "But I think your party will go a little more smoothly without my boys there to get into trouble."

"If you change your mind, you bring them. Christmas is for the children, no?"

Those words continued to echo in her mind as she said goodbye to Viviana a few moments later and hung up, then turned her attention to Jolie who was yawning in her high chair ready for her nap.

Her children certainly hadn't enjoyed the best of Christmases the past two years, but she refused to let them down this year. After tonight, she intended to relax and spend every moment of the holidays enjoying her time with them.

Perfect. It all had to be perfect. Was that such an unreasonable wish?

Her children deserved it. They had suffered so much pain and loss. Their last happy Christmas seemed like forever ago.

Joe had died the day after Christmas two years earlier, and they had known it was coming days earlier. No death of a man in his early thirties could be easy for his family to endure, but her husband's had been particularly tough. He had lingered in a coma for two months after the tractor accident, fighting off complication after complication.

Finally, just when she thought perhaps they had turned a corner and he was starting to improve, when she was certain his eyelids were fluttering in response to a squeeze of her hands or a particular tone of her voice, a virulent infection devastated his system. His battered body just couldn't fight anymore.

The next Christmas would have been hard enough for the boys, so close to the anniversary of their beloved father's death, but they had been forced to spend Christmas with Jenna's brother. Jolie, born five months after her father's death, had picked up a respiratory illness and had been in pediatric intensive care through the holidays, consuming Jenna with worry all over again. Then Pat, Joe's mother, suffered a severe stroke the week before Christmas, so Jenna had been running ragged between both of them.

This year *would* be different. Everyone was relatively healthy, even if Pat did still struggle with rehabilitation in the assisted-living center in Idaho Falls. Jenna's fledgling catering business was taking off and the sale of the Wagon Wheel had covered most of the huge pile of debt Joe had left behind.

She refused to allow anything to mess up this Christmas. Not a blizzard, not a big catering job she felt ill-equipped to handle, not sliding her car into a ditch.

Not even an arrogant neighbor with stunning blue eyes.

"You know you don't have to go to this shindig. I doubt anybody's expectin' you to. This was one of those, what do you call it, courtesy invites."

Carson made a face at his foreman, Neil Parker, as the two of them checked over his three pregnant mares, who were due to deliver in only a few months.

So far all was going well. This particular foal's sire was a champion cutting horse from the world-famous Dalton horse operation just up the road, and Carson had high hopes the foal would follow in his daddy's magnificent footsteps.

"I know that," he answered Neil. "If the local stock growers' association could have figured out a polite way *not* to invite me, I'm pretty sure we wouldn't be having this conversation."

"I doubt it's personal. You just represent change and a different way of lookin' at things, something that worries the old-timers around here. New West versus Old West."

Carson knew that. He knew his purchase of the vast acreage that used to be known as the Wagon Wheel had thrust him onto a hotly debated battleground. All across the West, old-guard ranchers were finding themselves saddled with land that was no longer profitable and practices that had become archaic and unwieldy.

Many of their children weren't interested in ranching and the lifestyle that came with it. At the same time, ranchers fought development and the idea of splitting the land they had poured their blood and sweat into tract subdivisions.

As feed costs went up and real-estate values plummeted, many were caught in a no-win situation.

He knew old-timers resented when new people moved in, especially those who had the capital to enact sweeping, costly changes in ranching practices in an effort to increase yield. It was even worse in his situation since he wasn't a permanent resident of his ranch and only came here a couple of times a month for a few days at a time.

He couldn't avoid the snide comments in town when he came to Pine Gulch. And he knew Neil suffered worse, though his foreman was careful not to share those details with him.

Neil and his wife Melina had been with Carson for a decade, first as caretakers of the central California ranch he purchased several years ago and then at the small Montana ranch he still owned.

Carson loved ranching. He loved being out on his horses, loved the wildness and the raw beauty here, loved the risk and the rewards.

It wasn't some big secret why that might be. That year he spent on his grandparents' ranch a few miles away from here had been the happiest, most secure of his life. He wasn't trying to recapture that, only to replicate it somewhere else if he could. And though Raven's Nest was only a small segment of his vast empire, this was where he found the most peace.

He wanted to make it a success and he figured a little proactive public relations couldn't hurt the situation in town. Life would be easier all the way around if Neil didn't have to play politics with obstinate locals.

"I'm not some Hollywood rancher, only looking for a status symbol. We're making something out of Raven's Nest and I need to get that point across. That's the whole reason I'm going to Viviana Cruz's party. You and I have been running Raven's Nest for ten months now and people still won't accept that we're serious about what we're doing here."

He thought of the coolness in Jenna Wheeler's eyes when he had pulled her van out of the snow a few hours earlier and the surprise she had showed when he had done the neighborly thing and told her he would make sure her driveway was shoveled.

He didn't know why her negative opinion of him bugged him so much. Plenty of people hated his guts. It was a normal side effect of both his position and his personality. He hadn't made McRaven Enterprises so successful by being weak and accommodating.

Jenna probably figured she had reason to resent him. He was radically changing something her husband's family had built over several generations.

He thought of what Hayden Wheeler had said the afternoon before. *He's the dude who stole our ranch.* Had the boy's mother been feeding him that kind of garbage? He didn't like thinking she would be the sort to come off as some kind of martyr. She had listed her ranch for sale and he had paid more than a fair price for it. End of story. It was a business deal, pure and simple.

Hell, he'd even made concessions, like granting her the right-of-way to use the Raven's Nest bridge and access road to the point where her driveway forked off it. Otherwise, she would have had to build a new road and another bridge across the creek, something costly and complicated.

He sighed and pushed the frustration away. What did it matter if she didn't like him? He certainly wasn't trying to win any popularity contests with Jenna.

It *would* be nice, though, if Neil didn't have to fight through the negative perceptions of everybody else in town every time his foreman needed to do business with anyone in the Teton Valley.

"I'm only going to go for a little while tonight," he said to Neil. "I'll shake a few hands, stroke a few egos and be home in time to make sure everything's ready for the guests coming in on Sunday."

"Hate to break it to you, boss, but showing up to one Christmas party with the cattlemen's association probably won't do much to change anyone's mind. Folks around here are set in their ways, afraid of anything that's different."

"What's to be afraid of? We're only trying to find more sustainable ways of doing business."

"You don't have to sell me, boss. I'm on board. I know what you're doing here and I'm all for it. Our overhead is about half of a typical ranch of the same size and the land is already healthier after less than a year. It's working. But what you're doing is fairly radical. You can't argue that. A lot of people think you're crazy to go without hormones, to calve in the summer, to move your cattle to a new grazing spot every couple of days instead of weeks. That kind of thinking isn't going to make you the most popular guy at the cattle growers' association."

"It can't hurt to let people see I don't intend to come out only on the weekends and hide out here at the ranch. I'm not trying to convert anybody, I just want folks to see I'm willing to step out and try to be part of the community."

"A noble effort, I guess."

"You don't mind if I tag along with you and Melina, then?"

"I suppose that would be okay. You want her to find you a

date? There's some real nice-lookin' girls around here who'd probably love to hit the town with a guy who has a private jet and one of them penthouses in San Francisco."

Carson narrowed his eyes at his foreman, whose sun-weathered features only grinned back at him. "Thanks, but no," Carson muttered. "I don't need help in the dating department."

"You change your mind, you let me know."

"Don't hold your breath. I'm not interested in a social life, just in a little public relations."

Chapter Three

Two hours later, he reminded himself of the conversation with his foreman as he listened to the Pine Gulch mayor ramble on about every single civic event planned for the coming year, from the Founders' Day parade to the Memorial Day breakfast to the annual tradition of decorating the town park for the holidays.

Public relations, he reminded himself. That was the only reason for his presence. If that meant expiring from boredom, it was a small price to pay.

"This is a nice town, as you'll find when you've been here a little longer," Mayor Wilson assured him. "A nice town full of real nice people. Why, I don't guess there's a more neighborly town in all of Idaho. You could have done a lot worse if you'd settled somewhere else."

"I'm sure that's true," he murmured to the other man, wondering when he could politely leave.

At least the mayor was willing to talk to him. He supposed he ought to be grateful for that. While he wasn't encountering outright hostility from people at the party, he had seen little of that neighborliness Mayor Wilson claimed. Most were polite to him but guarded, which was about what he expected.

The server walked past with more of those divine spinach rolls. He grabbed one as she passed by, hoping she wasn't keeping track of his consumption since he knew he'd had more than his share.

At least the food was good. Better than good, actually. He had come in with fairly low culinary expectations. A stock growers' holiday party in Pine Gulch, Idaho, wasn't exactly high on his list of places to find haute cuisine.

But the menu was imaginative and every dish prepared exactly right. He paid a Cordon Bleu–trained personal chef to fill his refrigerator and freezer here and in San Francisco and he thought the food at this party was every bit as good as anything Jean-Marc prepared.

None of it was fancy but everything he had tried so far exploded with taste, from the mini crab cakes with wild mushrooms to the caramel tart he'd tasted to the spinach rolls he couldn't get enough of.

He could only hope the personal chef he hired from Jackson Hole for the guests who were coming to Raven's Nest in a few days was half as good as this caterer.

The house party was an important one for McRaven Enterprises and he wanted everything to be exactly right, especially since he had a feeling this was his one and only chance to convince Frederick Hertzog and his son, Dierk, to sell their cellular phone manufacturing business to McRaven Enterprises.

Frederick loved all things Western. When Carson learned he and his family were traveling from Germany to Salt Lake City for a ski vacation, he had made arrangements to fly them to Raven's Nest for a few days in an effort to convince the man McRaven Enterprises was the best company to take Hertzog Communications and its vast network of holdings to the next level.

He and Hertzog had had a long discussion the last time they

met about some of the range policies Carson was trying to emphasize at Raven's Nest and the man was interested to see those efforts in action.

He expected to have more opportunities to entertain at Raven's Nest. He preferred his solitude while he was here but he had built the house knowing some degree of entertaining was inevitable. It wouldn't hurt to meet the caterer before he left, he decided. He could at least get a business card so he could pass it along to Carrianne, his enormously competent assistant who handled all his event-planning details.

The kitchen was at the rear of the community center. Just before he reached it, another server came through the doors carrying a tray laden with artfully arranged holiday sweets. Cookies and truffles and slices of nut bread.

He focused first on the food, wondering how upset she would be if he messed up her lovely tray by snatching one of those giant sugar cookies. He lifted his gaze to the server to ask and did a quick double take.

"Mrs. Wheeler!"

She wobbled a little and nearly dropped the entire platter. "Mr. McRaven," she exclaimed, in the same voice she might have used if an alien spaceship suddenly landed in the middle of the room. "What are you doing here?"

He raised an eyebrow. "I was invited. Why do you sound so surprised? This is the cattle growers' association holiday party, right? Since I run four hundred head of cattle at Raven's Nest, doesn't that make me eligible?"

She paused for only a moment and then continued to the buffet table, where she set down the tray before answering him. "Yes. Of course. I'm sorry. You certainly have the right to attend whatever party you'd care to. I just…wouldn't have expected you here, that's all. I was surprised to see you. The cattlemen's association is usually old-timers. The local good old boys."

"What about Viviana Cruz? You can't call her a good ole boy and she runs the whole association."

She smiled suddenly, brightly. "Point taken. Viv is definitely her own person. And we all love her for it."

With that smile, Jenna Wheeler suddenly looked as delicious as the food she was so carefully arranging, enough to make his mouth water. Her cheeks were flushed like the barest hint of color on August peaches and her silky blond hair was doing its best to escape the confines of the hair clip holding it away from her face.

He wondered what she would do if he reached out to finish the job, just for the sheer pleasure of watching it swing free, but he quickly squashed the inappropriate reaction. She was an extraordinarily lovely woman, he thought, not particularly thrilled that he couldn't seem to stop noticing that little fact about his neighbor.

"Are you helping the caterer tonight?" he asked.

She shrugged. "I guess you could say that. Is there something wrong with the food?"

"No. Quite the contrary. Everything has been perfect. I'm looking for a business card, in fact."

She blinked at him for a long moment, her big green eyes astonished, then she quickly looked away as if she hadn't heard him, her attention focused on arranging items on the buffet table for better access by the guests.

As the silence dragged on, he realized she wasn't going to respond. "So would you mind getting one for me from the caterer when you have a minute?" he pressed.

Again she gave him that odd look, as if she wasn't quite sure how to handle his request. Finally, she sighed and reached into the pocket of her red-and-green striped apron and pulled out a business card.

A nice touch for the caterer, he thought, to give all his servers business cards to be handed out upon request. He scanned it quickly, then felt his jaw drop.

Cold Creek Cuisine
Weddings, parties, reunions, or just an unforgettable, intimate dinner for two

Jenna Wheeler, owner

"You made all this?" he asked.

She gave him a long, cool look. "Why do you sound so surprised?" she parroted his own words back to him.

He had no good response to that, other than the obvious. "You're a widowed mother of four young children. Quite frankly, I'm astonished you have time to breathe, forget about running a business."

He didn't add that from what he had seen of her children, he would think just keeping them out of mischief would require six or seven strong-willed adults. Armed with cattle prods, for good measure.

"It can be challenging sometimes," she answered. "But I do most of the cooking when they're in school or sleeping."

Even when he came to Raven's Nest to relax, he could never completely escape work. Carson often had to take conference calls from Europe or Japan at odd hours. He remembered now that he had sometimes seen lights glowing at her house late at night and had wondered about it.

He was struck by another sudden memory. "Is that why you had so many groceries in your van today? I thought maybe you were just stocking up in case of a blizzard."

She laughed out loud and he was quite certain it was the loveliest sound he had heard in a long time. "My boys eat a lot, I'll grant you that. But not quite twenty grocery bags full. Yes, that's why I had so many groceries in my van. It was also the reason for my panic this morning. I had a million things to do before tonight and couldn't really afford the delay of being stupid enough to slide into a snowbank. Thank you again for pulling me out."

"You're welcome. I'm glad I was there. I would have hated missing all this delicious food. Your tandoori beef skewers are particularly wonderful. I don't think I've ever tasted anything like it."

"Thank you." She looked as surprised at the compliment as

if he had just reached over and kissed her hard, right here above the maple pepper salmon bites.

Not a completely unappealing idea, he had to admit.

None of this made sense to him. Not his sudden fierce attraction to her or the fact that she was here in the first place.

He had paid in the mid seven figures for her ranch, more than its appraised value because he hadn't wanted to quibble and risk missing out on the purchase after he had searched so long for the perfect rangeland for his and Neil's plans for sustainable ranching.

He would think with careful management, she and her children would be well-provided-for the rest of their lives.

But she drove a five-year-old minivan and her house needed painting and she worked after her children were in bed to throw parties for other people.

It was none of his business, he reminded himself. *She* was none of his business.

Except she *did* fix a mean goat-cheese crostini.

"Well, your food is fantastic. Do you mind if I give your card to my assistant who plans my events for me? I expect I'll be doing more entertaining at Raven's Nest in the future. I was hoping to find someone closer than Jackson Hole to handle the catering when I entertain. I never expected her to live just down the hill."

She paused for a long moment and he could clearly see the indecision in her eyes. He sensed she wanted to tell him no but instead she gave a short nod. "I suppose. I should warn you I'm very selective about the jobs I accept. If it doesn't work for my children's schedule, I have no qualms about turning something down. They come first."

"Fair enough."

He would have added more but the woman who had been helping Jenna serve at the party approached them at that moment. She barely looked at Carson but the quick glance she shot at him was icier, even more than Jenna's had been.

"Jenna, the mayor is asking if you have more of your bacon-wrapped shrimp. He's crazy about them, apparently. I told him I would ask."

"I'll have to go check the inventory in the kitchen." She turned toward Carson with an apologetic expression he wasn't completely certain was genuine.

"Will you excuse me? Things are a little hectic."

"Of course," he answered. He watched her go, not at all thrilled to realize the brief interaction with her had been the most enjoyable moments of his evening.

Why wouldn't the man just *leave* already?

Jenna returned to the kitchen after making yet another trip to replenish the buffet table, fighting the urge to bury her face in a pitcher of ice water.

This was becoming ridiculous.

She had made a half-dozen trips out into the holiday-bedecked community center, circulating among the guests with more cheesecake or toffee bites.

Every time, she had vowed to herself she wouldn't pay the slightest bit of attention to Carson McRaven. But the instant she would walk out of the kitchen, her gaze would unerringly find him, no matter where he was standing.

He shouldn't have stood out so glaringly. She had no reason to hone in on him like a heat-seeking missile. It wasn't like he was wearing some fancy tailored Italian-cut suit or anything. He had on perfectly appropriate khaki slacks and a light blue dress shirt under a sport jacket that looked casual but probably cost more than the average fall steer at market.

The man was just too blasted good-looking, with that dark wavy hair and those intense blue eyes. It didn't help that he wore his clothes with a careless elegance that was completely foreign compared to the off-the-rack crowd in Pine Gulch.

She couldn't help noticing him, maybe because he looked like a fierce hawk taking tea with a flock of starlings.

This is the cattle growers' association holiday party, right? Since I run four hundred head of cattle at Raven's Nest, doesn't that make me eligible?

If he was your average rancher, she was Julia Child.

"I can't believe that man had the nerve to show up here."

Jenna swiveled to find her sister-in-law coming through the doors with another empty tray. "What man?" she asked, playing innocent, just as if her thoughts hadn't revolved around him from the moment she had discovered him at the party.

"McRaven!" Terri's glare looked incongruous on her pixie features. "Does the man have to ruin everything? It's not enough that he waltzes away with your ranch and starts building that Taj Mahal on it but now he has to show up all over town like he owns the place."

"He didn't waltz away with anything, Terri. You know that. He paid good money for the ranch. And the house he built is big but it's not obscenely big."

"It's the biggest house in town. I mean, who really needs a twelve thousand square foot mansion out in the middle of freaking nowhere? Do you have any idea what kind of hit he's going to take if he ever tries to sell the place? Who else is going to want to shell out that kind of money in this soft market?"

"Does everything have to come down to real estate with you?"

Terri made a face. "I can't help it. I've got loan-to-values and escrow analyses on the brain."

When her sister-in-law wasn't helping her serve the mad rush of holiday events she had overcommitted to, Terri was studying for her real-estate license.

"McRaven should have taken a good look at the market around here before he jumped in and started building his mega-house," she added.

"I'm guessing he doesn't care about the market. He's got the money and the land. He's free to build whatever kind of house he wants on it."

She had to admit, she hadn't been thrilled that, for ten months, Raven's Nest had seen a constant stream of workers and delivery trucks and construction vehicles, with their dust and noise. The boys had been fascinated by it all but she had mostly found it annoying. And, okay, she had resented that Carson had the endlessly deep pockets to come in and make all the changes she and Joe had only ever been able to dream about in whispered conversations in the dark quiet of their bedroom.

"I still don't think it's right," Terri muttered. "He doesn't belong here. It doesn't help that he comes in looking like he just finished a photo shoot for some sexy men's magazine. No man should be allowed to be that rich and that unbelievably gorgeous. It's just not fair."

"You're a married woman, Terri!" she teased.

"Very happily married," she agreed. "But you have to agree, that man is lethal."

Jenna decided she would be wise to just keep her mouth shut right about now.

"You should see Annalee Kelley putting out the vibe. She's all over him. If Annalee has her way, she'll be the first one in town to see the inside of Raven's Nest. Or at least one of the bedrooms there."

Okay, she didn't want to go there, Jenna decided, and quickly changed the subject.

"How are the crab cakes? They seem to be going fast, don't they?"

Terri looked reluctant to be distracted but finally gave in. "You have, like, three left out there. You've done a fantastic job, as usual, Jen. Everybody's raving about how delicious the food is and at least a half-dozen people begged me for your white chocolate mousse recipe."

She had been working like crazy to make everything perfect for the party. It was amazing the sense of satisfaction she found.

"Thanks for all your help these last few weeks as everything has been so crazy, Terri. You've saved my bacon."

"You're welcome, hon. I'm just glad this is our last gig for a while. I can't wait for the cruise this week. I'm going to completely put the stupid real-estate test out of my head and just bask by the pool with an umbrella drink in my hand."

Her brother and his family were leaving the day before Christmas for a weeklong cruise on the Mexican Riviera.

"Well, I won't have umbrella drinks but I'll be glad to take a rest, too. It will be nice to have things get back to normal."

"As normal as your life can get when you live just down the hill from the McRaven McMansion. I heard from Melina Parker that he's got guests coming in this weekend. You let me know if there are any naked hot tub parties up there, okay? As much as I despise the man, I might have to come over with Paul's binoculars, just for a little peek."

Oh, as if she needed that visual image in her head. She thrust a platter at her sister-in-law to distract her. "Here. This is the last of the crostini. Try to move them. I don't want to take any home with me."

Terri grinned but obediently headed back out to the party.

The next time Jenna dared venture out of the kitchen, Carson McRaven was nowhere in sight. She told herself that odd, hollow feeling in her stomach was simply relief that he was gone and she could finally concentrate on the job at hand.

It certainly wasn't disappointment.

Chapter Four

"You've got company."

Carson looked up from his computer monitor. His foreman's wife, Melina—who served as housekeeper at Raven's Nest—stood in his doorway, a dust cloth in one hand and an amused smirk on her plump features.

"Can you handle it? This is not really a good time for me to be distracted. I'm videoconferencing with Carrianne right now."

Melina did a little finger wave. "Hi, Carrianne."

His hyperefficient assistant smiled from the computer screen. "Hello, Melina. How are you?"

"Can't complain. Except I woke up this morning with a little sciatica, but that should pass when this miserable cold weather eases a little. Sorry to disturb you two while you're plotting to take over the world or whatever, but I'm supposed to tell you that your visitors are on strict orders to talk to you and no one else."

"Who is it?"

"You'll have to find out yourself, won't you? See you, Carrianne."

Before Carson could protest, she grinned at him and at Carrianne on the computer screen then walked away. He frowned after her. Neither Melina nor Neil were the most docile of employees, which was probably the reason he liked them both so much.

"Is everything all right?" Carrianne asked.

"Damned if I know but I'd better go see. Can you hang tight for a few minutes?"

"Of course."

Even if some emergency kept him away all night and unable to reach her, he knew Carrianne would still be waiting by the computer for him in the morning. She was dependable to a fault—and invaluable for it.

The slightest of headaches thudded in his temples in rhythm with the frustration throbbing through him. He didn't need the distraction right now. He and Carrianne were trying to wrap up several projects before the holidays, a difficult enough task to accomplish via long distance. And even though Christmas was still five days away, the whole business community seemed to have decided to start celebrating early.

His frustration didn't ease when he reached the foyer and found the three Wheeler boys standing inside the doorway, snow dripping from their parkas onto his custom Italian tile floor. The oldest one, Hayden, he remembered, was holding a couple of small parcels.

Cold poured in from the door they had left open to the outside and he caught a glimpse of two ponies tied to the railing of the front porch. Two horses, three boys. Two must have been forced to double up, a fact he was quite certain didn't please either of them.

"Hi, Mr. McRaven." The medium-sized one with the glasses—Drew, he remembered—seemed to have been elected spokesman for the group.

"Hello, boys. What brings you up this way?"

"Our mom sent us." Apparently, Kip's trauma of a few days

earlier had been forgotten. He seemed to consider Carson his best friend, judging by the wattage of the gap-toothed grin he offered that should have looked ridiculous but seemed rather appealing instead.

"This is for you." Hayden barely looked at him as he thrust out the parcels and Carson now saw they were clear holiday patterned plastic containers filled with some kind of food items.

"We're supposed to tell you to put the spinach rolls in the refrigerator. The cookies you can leave out."

"I hope she gave you snickerdoodles," Kip said with that grin again. "They're my favorite."

"Okay." He had no idea how to respond to this unexpected visit or to their offerings.

"Tell him what we're supposed to say," Drew hissed to his older brother.

Hayden scowled, then spoke in a monotone. "We're supposed to tell you we're sorry for trespassing the other day and thank you for bringing Kip home when he fell off the fence and for pulling out our van yesterday when Mom got stuck in the snow."

"Uh, you're welcome." He had absolutely no experience with neighbors who thought they had to bring him cookies. It was a Mayberry moment he found unexpected and a bit surreal. Still, just the thought of having the chance to enjoy more of Jenna Wheeler's cooking made his mouth water.

"Your house is big," Kip said, looking around the two-story entry that led to the great room. "It's like a castle."

"Grandma Pat says it's a monster city up here." The oldest one stated the insult matter-of-factly. "She says you're only stroking your ego."

It took him a few moments to figure out "monster city" probably meant monstrosity. Either way, it annoyed him.

"Does she?" he asked evenly, wondering who the hell Grandma Pat might be.

Drew studied him, those green eyes behind the glasses wary. "Is that something mean? What Grandma Pat said?"

Again, Carson felt out of his depth and wondered the best way to usher his bothersome little visitors out the door. "I guess that depends."

"Grandma Pat says mean stuff like that all the time," he said, apology in his voice.

"She does not, moron. Shut up." Hayden punched his shoulder hard enough to make Drew wobble a little and Carson fought the urge to sit the boy down for a long lecture about not mistreating anybody, particularly smaller brothers.

Drew righted himself and stepped out of reach of his brother. "Mom says not to listen to her when she says something mean because she can't help it. She doesn't always think about what she's saying."

Hayden opened his mouth to defend Grandma Pat but before he could, Kip called out to them from inside the great room. "Hey, where's your Christmas tree?"

How had the kid wandered away so quickly? One minute he'd been there grinning at him, the next he was halfway across the house. Like wayward puppies, his brothers followed him and Carson had no choice but to head after them.

"Don't you have a tree?" Drew asked, his voice shocked.

"I have a little one in the family room off the kitchen." A four foot grapevine tree his interior designer had left at Thanksgiving, when he visited last.

"Can we see it?" Drew asked.

"Why don't you have a big one in here?" Hayden asked, with that inexplicable truculence in his voice.

"I guess I just haven't gotten around to it."

"Don't you like Christmas?" Kip asked, looking astonished at the very idea.

How did he explain to these innocent-looking boys that the magic of the holidays disappeared mighty damn fast when you lived in the backseat of your druggie mother's Chevy Vega?

"Sure, I like Christmas. I have a tree at my other house in California." One that his housekeeper there insisted on decorating, but he decided he didn't need to give the Wheeler boys that information. "I just haven't had time to put one up here. I've only been here a few days and I've had other things to do."

"We could help you cut one down." Drew's features sparkled with excitement. "We know where the good ones are. We always cut one down right by where the creek comes down and makes the big turn."

"Only this year we couldn't," Hayden muttered. "Mom said it would be stealing since it's on your land now. We had to go with our Uncle Paul to get one from the people selling them at his feed store. We couldn't find a good one, though. They were all scrawny."

The kid's beef was with his mother for selling the land, not with him, Carson reminded himself, even as he bristled.

"You want us to show you where the good trees are?" his brother asked eagerly.

"Drew," Hayden hissed.

"What? Maybe he doesn't know. It would be fun. Just like when we used to go with...with Dad."

The boy's voice wobbled a little on the last word and Carson's insides clenched. He didn't need a bunch of fatherless boys coming into his life, making him feel sorry for them and guilty that he'd had the effrontery to pay their mother a substantial sum to buy their family's ranch.

"We could take you on Peppy," the youngest beamed. "Peppy's the pony me and Drew share."

"Like three people can fit on Pep," Hayden scoffed. "He's so old, he can barely carry the two of you."

"Maybe he could ride his own horse," Drew suggested. "It's not far. So do you want us to help you? We already have our warm clothes on and everything."

"Don't be such a dork. Why would he want our help?"

Hayden's surliness and his brother's contrasting eagerness both tugged at something deep inside him, a tiny flicker of memory of the one Christmas he had been blessed to stay with his grandparents. He had been nine years old, trying to act as tough as Hayden. His grandfather had driven him on a snow-mobile to the Forest Service land above their small ranch and the two of them had gone off in search of a Christmas tree.

He had forgotten that moment, had buried the memory deep. But now it all came flooding back—the citrusy tang of the pine trees, the cold wind rushing past, the crunch of the snow under-foot. The sheer thrill of walking past tree after tree until he and his grandfather picked out the perfect one.

He could still remember the joy of hauling it back to his grandparents' home and the thrill as his grandmother had ex-claimed over it, proclaiming it to be the most beautiful tree they had ever had.

He and his grandfather had hung the lights later that night and he had helped put the decorations up. He had a sudden distinct memory of sneaking out of bed later that night and going out to the living room, plugging in the lights and lying under the tree, watching the flickering lights change from red to green to purple to gold and wondering if he had ever seen anything so magical.

The next Christmas, he had been back with his mother and had spent the holiday in a dingy apartment in Barstow. The only lights had been headlights on the interstate.

He pushed the memory aside and focused on the three boys watching him with varying expressions on their similar features.

He really did need a Christmas tree. It was a glaring omission, one he couldn't believe he hadn't caught before now when he had been trying to make sure every detail at Raven's Nest was perfect. He had guests coming in the next day who would be sure to wonder why he didn't have one.

He had no good explanation he could offer the Hertzogs, other than his own negligence. He just hadn't thought of it, since Christmas wasn't really even on his radar.

He didn't dislike the holidays, they were mostly just an in-convenience—a time when the whole world seemed to stop working, whether they celebrated Christmas or not.

On the other hand, where the hell was he going to get lights and decorations for a Christmas tree just five days before the holiday?

Carrianne could take care of that, he was quite certain. She would have the whole thing arranged in a few hours, even from California.

"You probably don't even know how to ride a horse, do you?" Hayden scoffed. "That's what Grandma Pat said. She says you probably don't know the back end of a horse from a hole in the ground."

Grandma Pat sounded like a real charmer.

"I do know how to ride a horse, thanks. I've been doing it for a long time now."

"You're just sayin' that."

He sighed at the boy's attitude. He never had been good at ignoring a dare. "Give me ten minutes to wrap some things up in my office, then you're welcome to judge for yourself whether I can ride or not. In the meantime, there's a telephone over there by the fireplace. Why don't you call your mother to ask her permission to go with me?"

The two younger boys couldn't have looked more excited than if he had just offered to let them fly his jet. Hayden, though, looked as if he were sucking on sour apples.

Yeah, kid, I know how you feel, Carson thought as he headed back to his study. He wasn't that thrilled about the whole situation, either. He should never have opened his mouth. He just had to hope Carrianne could arrange things so he wasn't stuck with a perfectly good evergreen he had cut down for nothing.

"You're doing what?"

Certain she couldn't possibly have heard Drew right, Jenna held the cordless phone closer to her ear and slid away from her sewing machine at the kitchen table and moved into the hall, where she could hear better without the whoosh of the dishwasher and the Christmas carols playing on the radio.

"Mr. McRaven doesn't have a Christmas tree," Drew said, in the same aghast tone of voice he might use to say the man kicked baby ducks for fun. "We told him where the good ones are, up above the far pasture, but that we couldn't go there this year to cut one down 'cause you said it was stealin'. But since it's his place now, it's not stealin' so he can get one there if he wants. And we're gonna help him."

Carson was taking her boys out to cut down a Christmas tree for his gigantic new house? Okay, what alternate universe had she tumbled into while she was sewing new pajamas for the boys?

Or maybe she fell asleep over the sewing machine and this was just some weird, twisted dream. He didn't like children and didn't know what to do with them. She didn't need him to voice the sentiment for her to figure it out. She had seen the vague uneasiness in his eyes every time he had been forced to extricate her boys from one scrape or another.

Why would he suddenly decide to take them to find a Christmas tree? It made no sense.

She shouldn't have sent them up to Raven's Nest, she fretted. She had thought the task would be an easy one and would accomplish a couple of purposes—reinforcing to the boys the lesson that it was good manners to express proper gratitude to those who helped them out for one. Getting them out of the house for a while and burning off a little pre-Christmas energy on their ponies was even better.

Now here they were heading off with Carson McRaven to cut down a Christmas tree.

Maybe she should just be grateful instead of worrying about his reasons. The boys had missed not cutting down their own tree this year. The one they found was perfectly adequate but Hayden in particular had been upset at any change in the tradition they had established years ago with their father.

"So can we go with him?"

"I don't think it's a good idea."

"Why not?" Drew, always the thinker, was never content with a simple answer.

How did she explain to her son that she was fairly certain their neighbor considered them on the same level as magpies or whistle pigs—an inescapable annoyance.

"I just don't. If he had truly wanted a Christmas tree, I'm sure he would have found one before now, don't you think?"

"He says he has one in his California house but hasn't had time to get one here since he's only been here a few days. Please, Mom. He needs our help. He said he could use it."

Really? Carson McRaven, cutthroat billionaire businessman said that? He could hire dozens of men to scour the mountainside for the perfect tree. What did he need with three mischievous little boys?

With those killer instincts all her boys had, Drew must have sensed she was wavering. "Please, Mom. Oh please. I promise, we'll be super good."

Jenna sighed. The truth was, she could use a little extra time. Jolie was taking a long nap and she had accomplished more in the last hour than she had done all day.

The pajamas she was working on were supposed to be a surprise on Christmas Eve—the boys' one present she allowed them to open early—and she still needed to finish hemming all three pairs. She enjoyed sewing but didn't have time for it very often. It seemed like every time she took out her machine, she had to relearn how to thread the bobbin and the rhythm of the thing.

What could be the harm in them going with Carson? He had made the offer, for some completely inexplicable reason.

"I suppose it's all right," she finally said. "Behave yourselves and come straight home when you're done."

"Thanks, Mom! Thanks a million! Bye."

Drew hung up before she could give more typical maternal admonishments. She set the cordless phone on the table but she couldn't quite bring herself to return to the sewing machine yet.

Her thoughts were still puzzling over why Carson McRaven would do something so incongruous as to invite her boys along on a tree-hunting trip.

Maybe it was the cookies she'd sent along with the boys to thank him for rescuing them the other day.

No, that couldn't be it. Sure, they were good but they weren't quite *that* good.

Drat the man, anyway. He was supposed to be hard and unfeeling and humorless. It was much easier to dislike him when she considered him simply an arrogant rich man who thought his money could buy anything he wanted.

But in the last few days, she could feel something changing. He had rescued her boys, he had pulled her out of the ditch, he had followed her home to make sure she was safe.

She was beginning to think there was more to Carson McRaven than she wanted to believe.

With another heavy sigh, she turned back to her sewing. Christmas was only five days away and she couldn't waste another moment obsessing about the man.

"That's the one, right there." The lenses of Drew's glasses gleamed in the sunlight as he beamed up at Carson from his spot standing proudly by a decent-sized blue spruce.

"That is a nice one," Carson agreed.

"This one's better," Hayden insisted from his spot by a gigantic lodgepole pine. "Yours has a big ugly hole on one side, see?"

"Well, *yours* is way too bushy," Drew retorted. "How do you think you're even gonna fit it into the house? It won't even go through the door!"

An excellent point, Carson wanted to say, but he decided to let them fight it out. He had one picked out already. He had it all figured out. It was just a matter of letting the boys wear themselves out arguing about it for a few more minutes, then he would present his tree as the winner.

In the course of the last half hour with the Wheeler boys, he had begun to finally determine which boy was which and to assess the dynamics between them. In the process, he gained a little more understanding.

Hayden, the oldest, wanted to be boss and was torn between pushing his weight around and trying to pretend he wasn't enjoying their little excursion. Carson knew it was small of him but he had savored the boy's reaction when he had led his favorite horse out of the barn, a high-spirited black named Bodie, and effortlessly mounted him. The boy had taken one look at the sleek, elegant lines of the magnificent horse and at Carson's easy control of him and his eyes had widened to the size of silver dollars.

Make sure you tell your Grandma Pat, Carson wanted to say, but that would have just been petty.

If Hayden had all the tough-guy attitude of the boys, his middle brother was the thinker. He seemed smart as a whip but also inordinately concerned with making sure everyone got along— except when it came to himself and his older brother, anyway.

Kip was eager to please and excited about everything, from the pair of pheasant roosters they scared on the way up the hill to the view of their house from that elevation.

"Here's one," Kip called now from some distance away. "What about this tree?"

"Let's take a look." Carson headed in the direction of the boy's voice and found him standing by the very tree he had already selected. It was a Douglas fir, with those soft, sweet-smelling needles, about sixteen feet tall, he judged, and in the perfect Christmas-tree shape.

"I think it's beautiful," Kip proclaimed.

"I have to agree with Kip on this one, boys. Good eye, kid. It's perfect."

"Thanks, Mr. McRaven!" The youngest Wheeler gave him that gap-toothed grin he found so appealing as his older brothers came to stand on either side of Carson.

Drew gave a wistful sigh. "It *is* perfect. Wish I'd seen it first."

"Are you kidding?" Hayden jeered, still determined to be the top dog. "It's too tall. You'll have to cut the top off."

"Not in my great room. The ceiling is eighteen feet high in there. This tree can't be more than sixteen, if that."

"If you say so."

"I do." He hid his amusement at the boy's determined reluctance to admit he might be wrong. "You want to help me do the honors?"

"What honors?"

Carson held up the small chain saw he had brought along and Hayden's green eyes widened with shock and the first flicker of excitement he had allowed himself to reveal. "Cut it down? You want me to help you?"

"If you're up to it."

"Can I help, too?" Kip's voice rose about two octaves in his exhilaration.

Carson hated to squash all that joyful anticipation but it couldn't be helped. He could just picture Jenna Wheeler's soft, lovely features if he returned one of her boys minus a few fingers.

"Not this time," he said, just as if there would ever be another time. "You and Drew need to stand clear. Go on back by the horses."

"Why does Hayden get to help and I don't?" Kip asked.

Carson raised an eyebrow in the same quelling look he gave to employees who pushed him a shade further than was wise. Kip didn't even notice.

"Huh? Why can't I help, too?"

"Because I said so," he answered. As soon as he heard his own words, he remembered all over again why he had always sworn he wouldn't have kids. He had absolutely no desire to become one of those adults who could only speak in clichés.

But he supposed clichés wouldn't be used if they didn't occasionally do the job. Kip gave a little huff of defeat and headed toward the horses, where Drew was already waiting.

"You know how to use a chain saw?" he asked Hayden.

"Don't you?" the boy asked, with just a trace of belligerence in his voice.

"Sure." He walked him through the steps and then started up the chain saw. The boy's eyes were bright with anticipation at the low throb as Carson guided the chain saw to the right spot on the Douglas fir's trunk.

"Now hold on tight," he ordered. The boy kept his hands on the chain saw, even as it bucked a little on a knot in the tree while they made the cut.

But as the tree toppled away from them, he gave a little shriek and instinctively pressed against Carson's side for just a moment. A weird knot formed in his throat but Carson swallowed it down.

"That was so cool!" Drew exclaimed.

"Yeah! Cool!" Kip echoed.

"Good job, Hayden," Carson told the boy.

"I could have done it by myself without any help," the boy answered, though Carson was quite sure he looked pleased.

"I'm sure you could," he answered.

"How are we going to get it to your house?" Drew asked with a sudden frown.

"I brought along plenty of rope. Bodie's strong enough to pull it down the hill, I think, especially since it's not far. He shouldn't have any problem."

The boys were more of a hindrance than they were a help as he rigged the rope but for once Carson didn't mind their chatter. It wasn't a bad way to spend a December afternoon, he decided. Not a bad way at all.

"If you want, we can help you set it up," Drew said as they finally headed back down the hill toward Raven's Nest.

"And we can decorate it, too," Kip added.

"We're really good at putting up Christmas ornaments," Drew said. "Mom said so."

"Yeah," added Kip. "This year I only broke one thing, a bell that I shook too hard. And it was really old anyway, Mom said."

Carson winced, as a sudden vision danced through his head of broken globes and tinsel strung across every available surface in his house. "Thanks for the offer, but I think it's taken care of. I've got some people who are going to help me with that."

Carrianne had assured him she should be able to have an army of decorators sent over from Jackson Hole as soon as possible. His guests weren't due to arrive until afternoon. By the time the Hertzogs arrived, his house should be brimming with Christmas spirit.

Thanks to the Wheeler brothers. If they hadn't showed up bearing their unexpected goodies, he would have completely overlooked putting up a tree. He owed them, he supposed. For that, and for the surprisingly enjoyable afternoon.

"We'll stop and let Bodie drop the tree off at my house and then I'll ride you all home."

He told himself quite firmly that he was only being neighborly, making sure they arrived home safely. The offer certainly had nothing to do with any desire on his part to see their mother again.

Chapter Five

Though cleaning out the horse stalls wasn't on her list of top ten enjoyable activities—or top five hundred, come to think of it—it had to be done. Since she'd finished sewing the pajamas and had safely hidden them in her secret spot in a locked closet in the basement furnace room where the boys never ventured, she had decided to tackle another job on her list.

She hummed "Jingle Bells" as she worked, much to Jolie's delight.

"Mommy funny," she pronounced with a giggle.

Jenna smiled. "Thanks, baby."

Even with her singing and Jolie's chatter and her horse Lucy whickering softly for a ride, everything seemed too quiet in the barn. Without the constant hubbub of her boys around, she always felt a little disconcerted, as if something wasn't quite right with her world.

They would be back all too soon, she knew, and then the chaos would start all over again. They would come in hungry and thirsty and arguing about whose turn it was to groom their ponies, Pep and Cola.

"Mommy, out," Jolie pouted from the playpen that wouldn't contain her for much longer. Jenna didn't like using it very often but a barn was a dangerous—not to mention less than sanitary—place for a busy toddler and she couldn't always keep a perfect eye on her.

"Just a minute, honey. Where's your car?"

"Jolie car."

"That's right. It's your car. Let's see it go vroom vroom."

Her daughter giggled again and picked up her plastic red car and let herself be distracted. She was such a good baby. Well, not a baby anymore. She was eighteen months old now, putting words together and walking and exploring her world.

She paused with the shovel in her hand, watching the miracle of her daughter as she babbled to her toys. She was a joy. A complete joy. The only tragedy was that her father had never seen his child, had never even known of her existence.

Jenna must have been only a few weeks pregnant at the time of Joe's accident. They had talked about having another child but hadn't yet made a final decision about it. Apparently fate had taken the choice out of their hands. And what a blessing that turned out to be.

Those first few weeks after the accident as he lay unresponsive in a coma, she had been so traumatized she hadn't even realized she was pregnant.

Oh, the signs had been there, just like in her other three pregnancies. She could see that now but at the time she had attributed her exhaustion and the missed periods to the stress of sitting by her husband's bedside day after day, praying for a miracle that never came as his condition continued to deteriorate. The vague nausea she had put down to lousy hospital food and not enough sleep as she rushed between the Wagon Wheel and the hospital day after day.

She found out for certain she was pregnant just a few days

after his funeral. New Year's Eve, and it was as if her husband had given her one last precious holiday gift.

Jolie had turned out to be her miracle. Even in the midst of her overwhelming grief—the paralyzing fear now that she was pregnant and on her own with a ranch to run and three little boys—she was forced to be strong for those boys and for the new life she carried.

Her daughter was a gift. All of their children were. Joe had loved them so. She knew he would have adored his little girl, would have spoiled her rotten.

"Mommy sad?" Jolie asked suddenly and Jenna realized she had stopped working and hadn't moved for several moments, just watching the wonder of her child.

"No, baby. I'm not sad." She smiled. "I'm happy. So happy. It's Christmas. The time of hope and love, right?"

"Santa!"

Her brothers had brainwashed her well. "That, too. Let's get this done so we can go inside where it's warm."

She had just laid down fresh straw when Frannie, their old border collie, lumbered to her feet and gave one sharp bark at the same time Lucy whinnied.

That was their not-so-subtle way of making Jenna feel guilty that they were stuck at home while the two ponies got to be out and about with the boys.

"I'm sorry, girls. I promise, I'll take you out one of these nights, okay? Just the three of us in the moonlight like we used to do."

The horse blew out a breath and Frannie just gave her a sad kind of look. Jolie giggled at her mother and Jenna picked her up and carried her outside to watch for the boys' return.

After the dim light inside the barn, the sunlight gleaming off the snow was blinding for a moment.

Just as she expected, she found her boys approaching the barn on Pep and Cola, Hayden on his own pony and Drew and Kip doubled up.

But to her vast shock, they weren't alone.

Her gaze took in the man on the huge, gorgeous black gelding. He looked like he'd just ridden out of a Clint Eastwood movie—black horse, black Stetson, dark green ranch jacket, all in stark contrast to the snowy landscape.

Her stomach did an odd little twirl and she hefted a squirming Jolie higher in her arms.

"Pretty horsie," the girl crowed with delight. Jenna had a sudden urge to warn her daughter to beware of pretty horses and the dangerous men who rode them.

"Hi, Mom!" Kip and Drew both greeted her with enthusiasm.

"Hi, guys. Hello, Mr. McRaven."

He nodded to her in greeting, his blue eyes gleaming brilliantly in the sunlight for just a moment, and with all her heart, she suddenly wished she hadn't just been mucking out the stalls. She felt at a distinct disadvantage around him, as usual. Just once she would like to encounter the man when she wasn't bedraggled and frustrated and looking like either a scullery maid or a stable urchin.

"How was the Christmas-tree hunt?" she asked.

"Christmas tree!" Jolie clapped her hands.

"We picked a huge one," Kip exclaimed, sliding down from behind Drew, who quickly joined him on the ground.

"We found the perfect tree," Drew added.

"*I* found the perfect tree," Kip bragged.

"Okay, Kip found it. It's perfect. And guess where we found it, Mom? Right in the place we always used to go, above the high pasture. Remember, Mom?"

"I remember," she murmured. As if she could forget eleven years of chopping down Christmas trees.

"It's perfect, isn't it, Mr. McRaven?"

"Pretty close," Carson answered.

"I still think it's too big," Hayden muttered. He climbed down off Cola, the pony his father had given him just a few months before his accident. "You're gonna have to cut off the whole top to get it inside your house, just like I told you."

"We'll have to see. If you're right, you have my permission to say *I told you so* as many times as you want. And next time I'll trust your judgment."

"I'm right. You'll see."

Hayden tugged his pony into the barn, much to Jenna's embarrassment. Her oldest son wasn't usually so rude. She could only hope he had exhibited better manners while he and his brothers had been with Carson.

As he was leaving, Carson gave the other boys a smile and said, "Thanks for your help. I never would have found the tree if not for the three of you."

"It was super fun." Kip grinned.

"Yeah, it was. We can help you find a tree again next year if you want," Drew offered.

Carson looked a bit taken aback by the offer. "Thanks. I appreciate that. Maybe next year I can remember to get a tree earlier than five days before Christmas."

"We can remind you," Drew assured him.

"Great. You do that." His gaze met Jenna's for just an instant but she could swear she felt the sizzle of it right to her toes. Ridiculous. She was holding her squirmy toddler and they were surrounded by horses and boys and one old, tired dog.

Still, when he dismounted and headed toward her, she couldn't help noticing his lean-hipped walk and the way his dark hair curled a little under the hat.

"I didn't know my buying the ranch would interfere with any of your holiday traditions," he said in a low voice that Drew and Kip couldn't hear.

She shrugged. "I knew when I sold the Wagon Wheel that many things would change. Our annual Christmas-tree hunt is the least of the changes."

He frowned. "But it's something your kids enjoy and I don't like being seen as the Grinch who deprived them of that."

"You didn't," she insisted, but he didn't look convinced.

"Look, there are plenty of trees up there, enough to supply

us both with Christmas trees for years to come," he said. "You and your family can consider yourself welcome to cut one of your own in the future."

She didn't quite know how to respond to his unexpected generosity. She also couldn't help thinking that even though he seemed uncomfortable making the suggestion, it was rather sweet of him to think of it. And very unlike the hard, implacable businessman she had always considered him to be.

"Thank you. But we found a great one this year, didn't we?" she asked the boys. "My brother Paul owns the feed store in town and he found us a really great one from the shipment he got this year. It's a balsam pine and it smells divine."

Kip and Drew nodded. "You should see how we decorated it," Kip said. "We made strings of popcorn and paper chains and lots of gingerbread-cookie ornaments. They smell super good, too. Only you can't eat them or you'll get sick, Mom says, because they're only decorations. Do you want to see it?"

"I saw it the other day when I brought you home, remember?"

"Oh, yeah." Kip looked disappointed at not being able to come up with another excuse to keep Carson around longer, and Jenna decided she had better step in.

"You boys need to take care of Pop. He's been working hard and is probably ready for a rest and some oats."

Neither of them looked excited at the chore but since they knew it was their responsibility and she wouldn't let them wiggle out of it, they sighed and trudged toward the barn doors, tugging the horse's reins behind them. Frannie hobbled up and followed them inside, leaving Jenna and Jolie alone with Carson.

"Hi, mister." Jolie beamed at him when the boys were gone and Carson gave her a slightly uneasy look.

"Hi," he answered.

"Pretty horsie," Jolie repeated.

"Uh, thanks."

The man looked as if he had no idea how to interact with a

little, blond curly-haired cherub. Jenna took pity on his discomfort and distracted Jolie by pulling out her wedding band that she kept on a chain around her neck. The diversion never failed to work and Jolie reached for it with an exclamation of glee.

While her daughter was busy jangling the necklace, swinging it back and forth and holding it up to catch the sunlight gleaming off the snow, she turned back to Carson. "I hope the boys weren't too much trouble."

"They weren't."

She couldn't help the laugh that escaped her, though she regretted it when he gave her an odd sort of look. "You don't have to sound so surprised," she said. "They *can* occasionally act like they're humans and not wild monkeys."

"They were fine. A few spats here and there but nothing too major. Actually, they were a big help finding the tree and it was...fun."

She had the feeling *fun* wasn't something Carson McRaven allowed himself to experience on a regular basis.

"I'm glad," she answered, then paused, remembering his unexpected offer of a few moments earlier. "Tell me they didn't lay some kind of guilt trip on you about our Christmas tree this year and having to find one in town instead of up on the mountain."

"No, not really. Except Hayden," he admitted. "He made a few disparaging comments about your tree being punier than usual."

She sighed. "Hayden would like everything to be the way it was before his father died. He misses him so much. All the boys do, but Joe and Hayden were extraordinarily close, I think because Hayden was the oldest."

"That's understandable."

"I guess you've figured out he's not happy I sold the ranch. He doesn't understand all the factors that went into the decision." She didn't add that Hayden was also close to his paternal grandmother, who was full of vitriol about Carson McRaven.

Pat's stroke had changed many things. Before it, Joe's mother had been sweet and loving, always willing to lend a hand to anyone in need.

Jenna had to constantly remind herself the brain damage from the stroke was to blame for the changes in Pat's personality now. She had transformed into an angry, bitter woman who sometimes took out her frustration at her physical condition on everyone around her.

"I'm sure it's tough for a kid to see someone else living at the place he always considered home."

"Maybe, but you own the Wagon Wheel now—sorry, Raven's Nest. You have every right to keep every single pine tree on it just as it is. You should feel no guilt or sense of obligation toward me or my family. About Christmas trees or anything else."

"It's all right, Jenna. I really don't mind. You're welcome to take any tree on the ranch next year. Hell, take two or three. We'll plant more."

She studied him for a long moment, trying to gauge his sincerity. He looked as if he meant every word. "Thank you. The boys will be thrilled. And I promise, we won't cut anything without asking permission of you—or of Neil Parker if you're not around. Though to be honest, I'd really like to get through this Christmas before I have to start worrying about next year."

"Fair enough." He returned her smile and she sternly ordered her nerves to stop jumping around just because the man looked devastatingly gorgeous when he wasn't being all tough and serious all the time.

He turned and mounted the horse in one fluid motion. "Tell the boys thanks again for their help this afternoon."

"I'll do that. Goodbye. And if we don't see you again before next week, Merry Christmas."

He studied her a moment and she was quite certain he wanted to say something else but he only touched a finger to the black brim of his hat, wheeled the horse around and cantered down the long drive toward Raven's Nest.

"Bye," Jolie called, somewhat sadly, and Jenna hugged her close, watching after him.

She didn't understand the man. He was hard and austere one moment, until she thought she had him pegged as a rather humorless businessmen only interested in his next deal. But then he showed these flashes of unexpected kindness to her and her family that completely baffled her.

"Mom. Mom!" Kip's dramatically raised voice rang out through the cold air. "Hayden says I'm too big of a baby to ever have my own pony. He says I'll have to share Pep with Drew forever. He's just lying, isn't he? Isn't he?"

She turned her attention to her boys, trying to put thoughts of Carson McRaven out of her head.

He was just her neighbor, a man from a completely different sphere than hers that certainly never involved mucking out stalls and wiping runny noses. Their respective universes would never have collided at all if she hadn't made the fateful decision to sell him the Wagon Wheel.

Three hours later, Raven's Nest rang with the sounds made by the team of designers Carrianne had rounded up, who were decking every hall and jingling every bell.

The tree he and the Wheeler boys had cut down and dragged back had indeed fit perfectly in his great room. The evergreen scent radiated even back to his office and he had to admit the big tree brought a nice, homey touch to the house he was certain the Hertzogs would appreciate.

Though right now as he talked once again via videoconference with Carrianne, he was tempted to call up Frederick Hertzog and cancel the family's entire visit.

"We have a contract," he said. "Sawyer agreed to provide two days' worth of meals while the Hertzogs are here. We have spent the last two weeks nailing down every single detail of the menu with him, down to the frigging after-dinner cheese assortment. Tell the man it's his responsibility to find someone to cover for him if he can't fulfill the terms of our agreement or we'll sue him for breach of contract."

Carrianne's normally serene features were decidedly flustered. "I told him that. You can be certain I was quite clear on our expectations. When vendors agree to do business with McRaven Enterprises, they need to be prepared to honor their commitments. Chef Sawyer assures me that he's tried everyone he knows. But this late in the season, anyone he can recommend in the Jackson Hole area is either taking the holiday off or is already completely booked."

"What are we supposed to do?" He refused to give in to the panic, though he was quite sure that whooshing he heard in his head was the sound of the entire deal heading down the toilet. "They're going to be here by lunchtime and I'm quite sure Frederick Hertzog and his family are expecting a little more than canned soup and tuna sandwiches, which is about all I can prepare."

Carrianne ran a hand through her hair, messing up a few strands, which was definitely a sign that she was upset. "I can check with your personal chef here in the Bay Area and see if he might be available to fly out under these special circumstances or if he can recommend anyone. You will, of course, have to make it worth their while."

"You can be damn sure I'll charge Michael Sawyer for the difference."

"You can hardly fault the man for needing an emergency appendectomy."

"Maybe not. But he should have a contingency plan in case of illness. It's just sound business sense to be prepared for every eventuality."

He thought he had covered all his bases for this visit. But perhaps they should have had a backup chef on standby.

"You know that even if I can find someone here in San Francisco, it's going to take some time to work out all the logistical details for them to travel to Pine Gulch, right? You might be on your own for lunch."

He grimaced, envisioning one nightmare scenario after another. "Just do what you can to get someone here as soon as possible, no matter the cost…"

His voice trailed off as he looked out his office window to the colored Christmas lights flickering in the twilight down the hill.

"Hold it. Wait a minute." He moved the curtain and looked down at Jenna Wheeler's house that seemed like a bright beacon against the wintry night. "Don't call anyone yet, Carrianne. I might be able to fix this mess after all."

"How?"

"Jenna Wheeler."

Carrianne frowned and looked down at something he couldn't see on the screen. "I don't think she's in my Contacts file."

"She wouldn't be. Jenna is my neighbor—the woman who sold me the ranch, remember?"

Carrianne made a sound of shock. "The one with the pestilent children? What does she have to do with any of this?"

Had he really said that about her children? After a few hours in their company, he regretted the harsh words. They weren't pestilent. Energetic and mischievous, maybe, but they were only boys. "Jenna Wheeler might just be able to salvage this situation, if she's willing, anyway. I'll let you know as soon as I talk to her. Just keep your fingers crossed."

Carrianne held up both hands, which were now as tangled as pretzels. "Consider it done," she said promptly.

But as he ended the call and headed for the door, Carson knew it would take more than crossed fingers to convince Jenna Wheeler to help him.

It might just take a Christmas miracle.

Chapter Six

"Can we open another one? Please, Mom? Just one more?"

She shook her head at Hayden, who was gazing at her with pleading eyes. "You know the rule. We only open one book each night until Christmas."

"But we have extras in the basket!" Drew protested. "Christmas Eve is in four more nights and we have six books left in the basket."

She should have known Drew would be the one to notice and point out that fact to his brothers. He would never let a detail like that slip past him.

"I know, honey. But I wrapped extras so we could read two or three books on Christmas Eve. Just in case certain people have a hard time falling asleep."

"Like Kip!" Hayden and Drew both said in unison and she laughed along with them. Her youngest boy was notorious for finding any excuse to stay up late, whether it was Christmas Eve or not.

"I'm not naming any names. But that's the reason for the extra books."

She had started a tradition when Hayden and Drew were barely old enough to sit still long enough for a story, of creating a storybook Advent basket. Each year she wrapped up all their old Christmas picture books in holiday paper and threw in a few new ones to surprise the boys. Every night from December first until Christmas Eve they were allowed to unwrap one book to read for their nightly story.

The tradition helped them countdown to Christmas and also provided Jenna an excuse to reread all their favorite stories. Even Hayden, who was now ten, still seemed to enjoy curling up on the couch by the fire while they read. It was a quiet, peaceful time in the midst of their usual chaotic day and Jenna savored every second.

"We've had our story, now off to bed. We'll open another book tomorrow."

The boys groaned and protested but she persevered and was herding them up the stairs toward their bedrooms when the doorbell suddenly echoed through the house.

"I'll get it!" Kip exclaimed, racing to beat his brothers in the mad dash to the front door.

Who could be knocking on their door this late? It was nearly nine p.m. Maybe one of their Cold Creek Canyon neighbors was out delivering cookie plates or something, she thought as she headed back down the stairs, hoping the doorbell didn't wake Jolie.

"Hi," she heard a deep voice say and her heart accelerated, though she knew that was wholly ridiculous.

"Hi!" Kip exclaimed. "Hey, Mom, look who it is! It's Mr. McRaven! Did you come to see our Christmas tree again?"

"No," he answered. "But now that I've had a good look at it again, I can verify that you were right, it is a nice one."

All three of her boys looked excited at Carson's visit, even Hayden, she saw with some surprise, though he was trying hard to hide it.

She had no idea why he might be there and he apparently had no inclination to immediately explain.

"Come in," Jenna said after an awkward moment. "It's bitter out tonight."

He took off his Stetson as he walked into the house and she fought the ridiculous urge to straighten his wavy hair that had been flattened a bit by the hat.

"It's started to snow again," he said. "There's already another inch or so out there. I guess we don't have to worry about a white Christmas, do we?"

She shook her head, but he still didn't move to enlighten her on his reason for stopping by. Her mind raced with possibilities but she discarded all of them.

"Is something wrong?" she finally asked.

His mouth tightened a little and she saw discomfort in his eyes. "You could say that. I need to ask a favor. A pretty big one."

"Do you need us to help you decorate your tree after all?" Drew asked eagerly.

Carson blinked at the boys in their pajamas. "Uh, no. I had people come do that today. But thanks for the offer."

He seemed so ill at ease, shifting his weight, curling his fingers around the brim of the hat he held, not meeting her gaze for longer than a few seconds at a time. Somehow Jenna sensed this conversation would be easier without the prying presence of three nosy little boys.

"Guys, to bed."

"Oh, Mom," Kip groaned. "We have company. Can't we stay up and talk to Mr. McRaven?"

"Not tonight," she said, her voice firm. "It's late and you've got chores and church in the morning. Come on, up you go."

They all three gave heavy, put-upon sighs but Jenna didn't waver. Apparently they saw she meant business. Though they didn't look thrilled about it, they trudged up the stairs at a turtle's pace.

"Drew, lights out means lights out. No flashlights under the covers so you can read a little more tonight, okay?"

His sigh was even heavier than his brothers' but he nodded and headed into the room he shared with Kip.

When she heard both doors close, she turned back to Carson. "Sorry. They're a little wired this time of year."

"Most kids are, aren't they?"

She nodded, then decided her curiosity couldn't wait another minute. "Sit down. You said you had a favor to ask."

He let out a breath and eased onto the sofa. "Not an easy thing for me, I'll admit."

She smiled, disarmed that he would confess such a thing. She knew exactly how hard it was to ask people for things. Since Joe died, she had tried to remain as self-reliant as possible but it wasn't always easy to do everything on her own.

"I'm in the midst of some…delicate negotiations to purchase a European company," Carson finally said. "I've invited the owner to stay at Raven's Nest for a few days while he's in the States for a ski vacation over the holidays with his family. He's flying up from Salt Lake City in the morning with his family. His wife, his son and daughter-in-law and his two grandchildren."

And this affected her and her family how? Jenna waited, still feeling completely in the dark. "Let me guess. You'd like me to keep the boys away from Raven's Nest while your guests are here."

His eyes widened and she was gratified that he looked completely startled at the suggestion. "No. Nothing like that. "

After another pause, he made a face and plunged forward. "The truth is, I hired a personal chef out of Jackson Hole to take care of the food while my guests are here. Michael Sawyer, with About Thyme Gourmet."

"He's a good choice. Probably the best you can find in the area." She knew the man casually from a few classes she had taken. While personally she found him to be an arrogant jerk, he was a fabulously creative chef.

"Only too bad for me, last night he was hit with acute appendicitis and he's in the hospital for at least two days."

"Oh. I'm sorry. Poor man. What an awful way to spend Christmas." She had firsthand experience how tough it was to be surrounded by hospital walls and beeping monitors and impersonal doctors during the holidays.

Carson blinked. "Right. It is unfortunate for him. But the fact remains that I still have guests arriving in a little over twelve hours and nothing whatsoever to serve them."

Suddenly everything made sense. She rose to her feet in a jerky motion. "No. No way. Absolutely not."

He raised a dark eyebrow. "How do you even know what I was going to ask?"

"What else? You want me to cook for your guests. And my answer is an unequivocal no."

"Why not?"

Could he really be this unbelievably arrogant, so outrageously self-deluded by the sense of his own importance? "It's four days before Christmas Eve, Carson. Did you forget that little detail? You honestly expect me to just drop everything at the last minute—my family, my own holiday plans—just so I can be at your beck and call?"

The heat of her response seemed to take him aback. He blinked at her with complete astonishment. "I'll make it worth your while. Whatever your usual fee would be for two days of work, I'll double it. No, triple it."

She was a professional, she reminded herself. Despite the weird currents between them and her ridiculous attraction to him, he was a potential client offering her a lucrative position. One that might have long-ranging benefits if he was happy with her work and continued to use her for Raven's Nest events.

But before she was a caterer, she was a mother and that had to come first. "I can't leave my children this close to Christmas. I just can't, Carson. We've made plans. I told them the stockmen's party was my last event of the season and I can't break my promise."

"It's just for a few days."

"Which can seem like a lifetime to children. I promised myself I wouldn't let anything ruin their holiday. Not this year."

"Why not? What's so important about this year?"

"You wouldn't ask that question if you had children of your own."

A weird expression flitted across his features but it was gone so quickly she thought she must have imagined it.

"Every year is important when you have children. This is the only time in their lives they'll be ten, eight, six and eighteen months. Next year will be an entirely different dynamic. Time marches on. If I learned anything from Joe's death it's the importance of magnifying every moment I have with my children."

"A lovely philosophy in the abstract. But we're only talking about two days."

"I owe them. Don't you see? We haven't had the best holidays for the past years. Two years ago, their father was dying and we were dealing with the funeral arrangements and everything. Then last year, Jolie, my little girl, was in the hospital with pneumonia. The boys had to spend Christmas with their aunt and uncle while I was at the hospital with her for most of the holidays. I promised them—and myself—this year would be different."

"It's only for a couple of days," he repeated. "You'll still have Christmas Eve and Christmas Day and the whole rest of the holidays."

She had a feeling she could argue with him until her ears turned blue but he wouldn't understand. "No. I'm sorry, but you'll just have to find someone else."

He rose to stand in front of her and she was caught by the plea in his blue eyes. "There is no one else, Jenna. Not at this late date, not this close to Christmas. Look, I'm desperate. This visit with Frederick Hertzog and his family is important to me."

"And my children are important to me, Mr. McRaven. Far more important than any business deal."

* * *

He gazed at her, with her holiday-red sweater and her plain gold hoop earrings and her honey-blond hair piled up on top of her head in a haphazard way that should have looked a mess but somehow managed to look tousled and pretty.

How could she appear so soft and fragile yet be so maddeningly stubborn at the same time?

He considered his options. None of them were very palatable. The idea of serving macaroni and cheese from a box for every meal filled him with cold dread. He supposed he could order in every meal but the restaurant options in Pine Gulch weren't exactly gourmet, either. The coffee shop served decent, honest food but nothing memorable.

There were good restaurants in Jackson Hole or Idaho Falls but both of them were at least forty-five minutes away in opposite directions. A little too far for a quick to-go pickup.

No, Jenna Wheeler was his best alternative. Now if only he could make her realize how limited his choices were.

He narrowed his gaze and tried a little hardball. "You know, I could always decide to lock the gate to the bridge across the creek. It belongs to me now and there was nothing in our sale agreement that obligated me to provide access to you or your family."

She stared at him, sudden fury kindling in her gaze, and he realized the soft little kitten had sharp claws. "You would really go to such lengths to get your way?"

He sighed, not sure whether he despised himself more for making the suggestion in the first place or because he didn't have the stomach to follow through on it. "Probably not," he admitted. "But I am in dire straits here, Jenna. What about just helping me out with brunch and dinner tomorrow? That would at least give my people time to fly someone else in from the Bay Area for the second day."

She raked a hand through her hair. "I promised the boys we would go sledding after church tomorrow."

"You could still do that, in between meals."

"You have no idea how long it takes to prepare a halfway decent meal of the scope you're talking about, do you?"

"Not really. I'm not much of a cook, I'm afraid. You make it seem effortless, though."

"Effortless. Right." She shook her head but he could sense she was wavering.

"Please, Jenna." He pushed a little harder. "If you do this for me, I promise, I'll never again bring up the idea of you selling the rest of your land to me. I'll never get mad at your boys for wandering where they're not supposed to be. I'll be the perfect neighbor."

"Ha."

Her cynical exclamation was in such contrast to her soft prettiness that he had to laugh.

"I swear it."

She sighed heavily. "How many guests did you say you were expecting?"

"Six total. Frederick and Antonia Hertzog, their son, Dierk, and his wife, Elle, and their children Amalia and Gregor. They have no food allergies, though Gregor doesn't like anything with onions and Elle insists on low saturated fats."

"What sort of menus have you discussed?"

"I can provide you with everything Sawyer had talked to my assistant about before his unfortunate medical complications. But you don't have to feel obligated to follow his plan. I can be flexible."

This time her laugh was filled with unabashed doubt. "*Can* you? I believe I would like to see proof of that."

Her tart tone made him smile. "I can. Just watch me."

She gave him a long, considering look and he wondered what was going on behind those lovely green eyes.

"So does that mean you'll do it?"

She sighed. "How can I refuse for three times my regular rate and your promise that you won't nag me to sell the Wagon Wheel to you anymore?"

He winced. "You're going to hold me to that, I suppose."

"That's the only reason I would even consider it."

"And people call me a merciless negotiator."

"I'll need your assistant to fax me copies of all the menus tonight and a complete inventory list of the food items Michael Sawyer has already purchased. I may need to make some changes if he was planning dishes I can't fix."

Was that enthusiasm or nerves he could see sparking in her eyes? Whatever it was, she looked bright and vibrant and extraordinarily lovely.

"You can fix anything you'd like," he finally said. "I completely trust your judgment."

Her mouth tightened and the spark went out as if someone had dumped a foot of snow on her. "No, you don't. You think I'm a terrible mother who can't control her own children."

He stared, genuinely astonished. "When did I ever say that?"

"You didn't have to say the words, Carson. Every time the boys have gotten into trouble on your property and we've had to discuss it, I've seen the reaction in your eyes. You try to hide it but I know you find them frustrating."

Only a few days ago, he would have wholeheartedly agreed with her. But something had changed in the last day or so. He couldn't put his finger on it but he didn't find Jenna Wheeler and her family nearly the abhorrent neighbors he once had.

"They're growing on me," he admitted.

She tilted her head and studied him for a long moment then she smiled. "Good. Because I'm not sure I'll be able to find child care tomorrow morning. If you insist on me cooking for your guests, you just may have to deal with my children coming along to Raven's Nest with me, as well."

For just an instant, panic spurted through him at the idea of three active boys and a toddler racing through his mountaintop haven, knocking over priceless antiques, pressing sticky hand-prints all over the walls, asking him endless questions he didn't know how to answer.

He squashed it quickly. She was doing him a huge favor and he couldn't quibble about her terms.

Chapter Seven

With a vague sense that she was stuck in some weird dream, Jenna entered the kitchen at Raven's Nest just after 7:00 a.m., four hours before the guests were due to arrive.

She was already cursing whatever ridiculous impulse had convinced her to help Carson.

This was crazy. She had no business being here when she still had presents to wrap, a few last-minute stocking stuffers to find and the guest room to dig out for Pat's annual Christmas Eve visit.

And where was she? Standing in a room that looked as if it were straight out of the pages of some kitchen design magazine.

If she needed yet another reminder of all the differences between the two of them, she only had to look at his kitchen. It was a dream of a room, exactly how she would have laid out her own fantasy kitchen—wide marble countertops, an efficient work space in the middle, double refrigerators, six-burner professional-grade cooktop, even a wok station. He had everything she could have fantasized about.

Ironic that a man who claimed he didn't cook would have the most gorgeous kitchen she had ever seen. But she supposed she shouldn't be surprised. Carson McRaven struck her as a man of impeccable taste. He wouldn't build a house like Raven's Nest, with its soaring views and careful attention to style and elegance, and stick a subpar kitchen in the middle of it.

Jenna moved to the window, where the only building she could see was her own house, its white paint blending into the snow. The house she loved so much looked humble and rather shabby from this vantage point. Was that what Carson thought when he saw it?

She gripped the sink's edge as sudden panic assailed her. She had no business being here. This was a huge mistake. Someone's idea of a cosmic joke.

What did she know about cooking for people who flew on private jets and had kitchen appliances that probably cost more than her van, even when it had been new?

Breathe, she ordered herself. *You can do this.*

She was on her third round of circle breathing, focusing on her house and the love and laughter she found in it, when she sensed she was no longer alone. She turned and found Carson standing in the doorway watching her. He wore jeans and scuffed boots and a Western shirt and looked as if he would have been more at home herding strays in the high country or slinging longnecks down at The Bandito than standing in this beautiful kitchen with the morning sunlight slanting across his features.

"Morning," he said. "Melina just told me she let you in. Are you ready for this?"

"Wrong question." She did her best to keep the alarm that bubbled through her from filtering into her voice. "I was just thinking I'm not sure I can pull this off."

One corner of his mouth lifted in a devastating smile. "Of course you can. I've tasted your food, remember? Everything you served at the stock growers' party was delicious and I think I finished off what your boys brought over the other day in about half an hour. You're brilliant in the kitchen."

"Brilliant? I wouldn't go that far."

"I wouldn't have asked you to do this if I didn't think you could handle it, Jenna. You should know that."

His words steadied her and she took one more deep breath and pushed the panic away.

"Is everything on schedule, then?"

He nodded. "I'm meeting the Hertzogs' plane in Jackson at ten. I was just about to head out but I wanted to check in with you first. Do you have everything you need?"

She glanced around the gleaming kitchen and almost laughed, though she was afraid if she started, she would end up in hysterics and he would have to cart her away.

What could she possibly need that wasn't contained in this chef's paradise? "I should be fine. According to the inventory Carrianne faxed me last night, I should have enough food to feed several dozen people for a couple of weeks."

"In a couple of weeks, I'll be back in San Francisco and my company will, knock wood, be the proud owners of Hertzog Communications."

"Unless I screw up and poison everyone today."

He laughed. "Try not to do that, okay? Call me if you can't find something you need and I'll try to pick it up while I'm in town."

"Don't you pay people to fetch and carry for you?" she asked. "I would think Carson McRaven of McRaven Enterprises would be too busy for airport runs and hitting the grocery store."

He hesitated for a moment then nodded. "Yeah, I could send someone to pick them up. But Frederick Hertzog is the sort of man who appreciates the personal touch. A few hours out of my schedule is a small price to pay if it helps convince him McRaven Enterprises will take good care of the company his family built over three generations, first as a telegraph company, then telephones, and now cells."

No wonder the man had created a huge dynasty in such a short time, if he used that sort of sound business sense in all of his dealings.

"I really owe you for this, Jenna."

She gave him a dark look. "Yes. You do. I'm blaming you if my children's Christmas is ruined because their mother had a nervous breakdown."

His laugh was warm and amused and sent chills rippling down her spine. "And where are your children this morning? I thought they would be belly flopping into the swimming pool by now."

"You caught a very lucky break. My sister-in-law called last night after you left and asked if they could come over today and help her make gingerbread houses. When I told her what I was doing for you, she insisted on taking them to church and then having them spend the afternoon with her. My niece will watch them this evening and then again tomorrow. And you're paying them an outrageous amount for it, by the way."

"Am I? Good for me."

She couldn't contain the laugh that escaped her. It helped ease the tension gripping her shoulders like an eagle's talons—until he smiled back at her and her insides felt as if she had just taken a free fall from the Grand Teton.

She quickly looked away and her gaze rested on one of the small appliances she hadn't noticed before. "Oh, my word. You've got a steam oven! I've been dying to try one of these."

"Well, here's your chance."

He studied her for a long moment and there was a strange light in his eyes at her excitement, something glittery and bright. A thin, tensile current tugged between them and she couldn't seem to look away.

He was the first one to break eye contact. He cleared his throat and eased away from the counter. "I'd better get moving. Give me a call if you find you're in need of anything else."

"I'll do that." To her dismay, her voice sounded raspy and hollow.

After he left, she stood for a moment, wondering what on earth that was all about. This attraction was completely absurd, she reminded herself. She had no business even thinking about Carson McRaven that way.

His kitchen. That was another story entirely. Any normal, breathing foodie would salivate buckets over this kitchen.

She had the tools, she had the ingredients. Now she just had to do them all justice.

Despite the pep talk she gave herself and the vague comfort she found in knowing Carson had faith in her, nervous tension still seethed and simmered in her stomach all morning as she worked alone in the Raven's Nest kitchen.

As the huge black-rimmed clock over the fireplace ticked inexorably away, that tension grew to full-blown panic. She had pulled out the last batch of cinnamon apple muffins and was stirring the light mushroom sauce for the chicken crepes when she heard a commotion outside the kitchen.

"Sounds like our guests are here," Melina Parker said from the other side of the kitchen, where Jenna had, with desperate gratitude, taken up her offer of help by enlisting her to finish cutting pineapple for the fruit plate.

Nerves jumped inside her but she forced herself to focus on the work at hand. "Thanks again for helping me. I'm afraid I wouldn't even be close if not for you."

"No problem. I can handle slicing and dicing, as long as I don't have to come up with menus or use any creativity," Melina answered. "What else can I do?"

Jenna looked around the kitchen, which was a great deal more disorganized than it had been when she first walked into it three hours ago. "I think the smoked salmon eggs Benedict is ready. And these crepes are just about done. You could take them out to the buffet table, if you don't mind."

"That's why I'm here, darlin'."

Melina headed out of the kitchen with her arms full. When Jenna heard someone come back inside a few moments later, she assumed it was Carson's housekeeper and didn't turn around.

She was too busy taking the pineapple-glazed ham out of the oven. "Can you put a few more of the banana-walnut muffins in the basket and take out a couple of the blueberry to even the numbers a little more?"

"Um, sure."

At the unexpected deep voice, she swiveled her head and found Carson standing in the doorway.

"Oh. Sorry. I thought you were Melina."

"I'm not. But I don't mind rearranging your muffins for you."

"You don't have to," she protested. But he had already crossed to the prep sink on the island to wash his hands.

"How's everything going in here?"

Even though he was stepping in to help, she couldn't control her glare. "That reminds me. Go away. I'm not talking to you right now."

He laughed and she found it terribly unfair that even in the midst of the kitchen chaos and her own personal crisis, he could still make her pulse jump.

"The entire house smells fantastic. If everything tastes even a tenth as good as it smells, you have absolutely nothing to worry about."

"Easy for you to say. They're European!"

"What does that have to do with anything?"

"European jet-setters. They probably have their own personal chef trained at Le Cordon Bleu. Do you know where I was trained? Do you?"

"No idea. Where?"

"The greasy-spoon diner in town. Yes, I received a degree in food sciences but all my practical experiences came from Lou Archeleta, the cook at the diner. I worked there all through high school and he sometimes let me try out new dishes. Oh, this is going to be a disaster."

"Jenna, relax."

He stepped closer and rested a hand on her shoulder. For one crazy moment, she wanted to close her eyes and just soak up the comfort he offered. The strength of the impulse astounded her. It had been so very long since she had anyone to lean on.

At least since Joe's accident. Longer, she supposed. He had been so busy working fourteen- and sixteen-hour days trying to hang on to the ranch that she had learned early in their marriage to be self-sufficient.

Right now the idea of sharing her burdens with someone else for a moment seemed a seductive temptation.

"Everything will be fine." Carson squeezed her shoulder. "I think you'll like the Hertzogs. They're warm and friendly and not at all pretentious. Your food is going to wow them. Trust me."

She wanted to. Oh, she wanted to. Right now it was difficult to remember their relationship was strictly that of neighbors and now client and chef.

Difficult but not impossible, she reminded herself and made a concerted effort to step away from his enticing heat and strength, using the excuse that the cottage potatoes had to be stirred one last time before she transferred them to a serving bowl.

"I guess we're about to find out, aren't we?" she murmured, then arranged a garnish on the potatoes, picked up the serving bowl like a shield and headed into the dining room.

"What a spectacular view you have here. If I had a home here, I would never want to leave it." Antonia Hertzog smiled at him and Carson wondered why she reminded him so forcefully of his grandmother.

The two women were nothing alike. His grandmother, God bless her, had been short and stout, with broad, sun-baked features and wavy gray hair she kept in a ruthless hairnet. Antonia was slender with ageless features and that innate élan that seemed so effortless in European women.

Still, something about the warmth in her eyes brought his grandmother firmly to mind.

"I fell for the view the first time I saw it," he admitted. He didn't add that very few other places in his life had given him such an instant connection. His grandparents' ranch had felt the same but he supposed his chaotic, nomadic upbringing made it more difficult for him to feel so at home in any particular place.

"I can see why," she answered. "Do you spend much time here?"

"Not as much as I'd like. The house has only been done for a short time. I expect to get away from San Francisco more often in the future."

"A man cannot work all the time," Frederick said, with a meaningful look at his son, Dierk, who was too busy sending a message on one of the company's cutting-edge phones to even notice.

"When may we ride the horses?" Dierk's son, Gregor, asked. Gregor was twelve, two years older than his sister, Amalia, who hadn't said more than a word or two throughout the entire delectable meal.

"That's up to your parents. After brunch would be fine with me."

"May we, Mother?" Amalia asked, her tone as formal as if she were petitioning the queen for a stay of execution.

"You both must have a rest first." Elle Hertzog was as whip-thin as a greyhound and though Jenna's food was divine, she had eaten only a little fruit and half a muffin. "We have already had a rather long morning."

Carson expected protests but both children only nodded solemnly. In his limited experience of children, he couldn't help contrasting the behavior of Amalia and Gregor to the Wheelers. The Hertzog children had impeccable table manners and didn't so much as fidget on their chairs.

He imagined Jenna's boys would have been swinging from the chandelier right about now. They were noisy and busy and troublesome. He wasn't sure why he found their spirited antics so much more appealing.

* * *

After their meal, he stayed out of the kitchen as long as he could manage.

The Hertzogs opted to go in their rooms for a short time to unpack and relax before their scheduled afternoon ride, leaving him feeling rather disjointed and at loose ends.

He had a great deal of work he could be doing. Contracts to study, phone calls to make, reports to read.

All of that paled in comparison with the insistent tug he felt toward Jenna Wheeler.

For the life of him, he couldn't understand his powerful attraction to her and he wasn't sure he liked it. Certainly she was a lovely woman, with those stunning green eyes and her soft blond hair and delicate features. He was surrounded by beautiful women all the time, but none of them fascinated him as she did.

He rationalized his trip back to the kitchen by reminding himself that before brunch she had been as nervous as a long-tailed cat at a hoedown, to use one of his grandfather's favorite phrases.

Didn't he owe it to her to set her mind at ease? To reassure her that the food had been devoured by the Hertzogs, who commented several times on how delicious it was?

Only for a moment, he told himself. He could compliment her food, thank her again for helping him, then return to his office in only a few minutes and tackle his workload.

He heard her before he saw her. Her low contralto voice sang a quiet Christmas carol that somehow sounded more lovely in this setting than the opera diva he had been privileged to hear a few weeks earlier in San Francisco.

He stood in the hallway outside the kitchen and let the sweetness of the song wash over him, of babies and mangers and a hope for the future.

When her song ended, he took a couple of breaths then walked into the kitchen, acting as if he had just come from another part of the house. He didn't think she would appreciate knowing he had spied on her for the last five minutes, at least aurally.

At his entrance, she looked up from stirring something in a bowl. "Oh. Hello."

He forced a smile, not at all sure why his chest suddenly ached. "I knew you were good. I didn't realize your food would be the hit of the day so far."

"It was okay, then?" she asked, then winced. "Forget I said that. I swore to myself I wouldn't ask."

"Why not?"

She shrugged and turned back to the mixing bowl. "I'm quite certain you'll tell me if the meals I prepare don't meet your lofty expectations."

"Do I come across as such an ogre, then?"

He meant it as an off-handed comment and didn't really expect a response but she frowned, appearing to give the matter serious consideration. "Not an ogre. Not at all. Just a man who demands perfection. Or as close to it as we mortals can provide."

"In that case, my expectations were far exceeded. Brunch was absolute perfection. Far better, I'm sure, than Michael Sawyer would have provided."

Her smile took his breath away and made that ache return to his chest. "Thank you, Carson. I'm so glad you enjoyed it."

"I wasn't the only one. Frederick and his wife both commented on how delicious the food was."

She smiled again. "I can't tell you what a huge relief that is to hear. Now maybe I can relax a little for dinner."

He suddenly wanted fiercely to kiss away those nerves. The impulse shocked the hell out of him and he moved away a little, using the excuse of going to the refrigerator for a bottle of water.

"Did you have the chance to use the steam oven?" he asked. He knew he ought to leave now but he couldn't quite bring himself to walk out of the warm, fragrant kitchen.

"I did. It was incredible. I steamed the mini Christmas puddings in it. I've never had them turn out so well."

She glowed with excitement as she talked about cooking. He had never known anyone to get so thrilled about Christmas pudding and he had to admit, he found her fascinating. Refreshing.

"I'm glad it worked out."

"I'm going to bake the bread for tonight in it. I can't wait to see how it works. It's supposed to leave the crust hard but the inside perfectly soft."

"You're making the bread?" It was a completely foreign concept to him.

"Of course. You didn't expect me to serve plain old Wonder to your guests, did you? They're European!"

He couldn't help himself, he laughed out loud. For just an instant, her gaze shifted down to his mouth and suddenly the air changed. Those currents started zinging between them again and a blush crept up her cheeks.

He wondered what she was thinking about that turned her skin that lovely rose. And why was she staring at his mouth?

He wanted to kiss her. The impulse took him completely by surprise. He wanted to take Jenna Wheeler in his arms and kiss her right here in this kitchen smelling of cinnamon and spice and everything nice.

He told himself he couldn't do it. She wasn't interested in a kiss—or anything else—and she would probably slap him if he tried.

But maybe not.

He probably could have just backed out of the kitchen and left her to her steam-oven bread baking. But just at that moment, she stirred the contents of the bowl she was holding just a little too hard and the whole thing started to slip out of her hands. He was close enough to lunge after it and for a moment, they both stood together holding the bowl between them.

He could feel the heat of her, the suppressed energy, and

again her gaze flicked to his mouth. He knew he should back away but she was so soft and curvy against him and her mouth was right there and his sudden fierce hunger to taste that soft mouth was more than he could control.

Chapter Eight

She had forgotten what an intense physical experience a kiss could be. Though he touched her with only his mouth, her entire body seemed to sizzle to life, as if all that made her female had been lying dormant since her husband's death.

Every sense seemed heightened, superacute. She could hear the blood pulsing through her veins, the ragged sound of his breathing, could feel his heat seeping into her muscles. He smelled divine, a sensuous mix of laundry soap and a subtle aftershave with notes of bergamot and something woodsy and masculine.

As wonderful as he smelled, he tasted even better, of coffee and cinnamon and something elusive she couldn't identify.

It was an addictive mix, sultry and seductive, and she felt ridiculously like a banana flambé, as if everything inside her was being caramelized and sweetened by his touch.

The most alluring part was that when she was in his arms she didn't feel like a young widow or like somebody's mother. She was only Jenna, a woman who had dreams and hopes and desires of her own.

As he lingered at her mouth, licking at the corner, tasting and teasing, she lost all sense of time and whatever tiny ounce of common sense she might have possessed before he walked into the kitchen.

Oh, it had been far too long. She had forgotten the way a man's touch could make her head spin and her insides flip around with wild joy. She had forgotten the churn of her blood and the yearning heat that stirred up out of nowhere like a dust devil on a July afternoon.

Somehow she was no longer holding the mixing bowl, though she wasn't sure if he had set it on the counter or if she had. Whoever had done it, with her hands free now she couldn't resist wrapping her arms around the strong, tanned column of his neck. She wanted to burrow against him, to absorb his strength inside her.

As the kiss continued, other sensations gradually pushed their way to the forefront of her consciousness. The slow, resolute tick of the big clock above the fireplace, the hard marble countertop pressing into the small of her back, the quiet whoosh of the dishwasher.

What on earth was she doing here? She hadn't touched a man in two years and here she was tangling tongues with Carson McRaven, of all people.

Yes, he was gorgeous and any woman would probably be thrilled to find herself in Jenna's comfortable-soled sneakers right about now.

On a physical level, she couldn't deny she was fiercely attracted to him. But could she have picked a worse male on the planet to grab on to for her jump back into the whole man-woman scene?

Carson was coolly arrogant, used to getting his own way at any cost. Worse than that, he disliked children. Especially *her* children.

She had to stop this somehow. She summoned all her strength and wrenched her mouth from his. With the countertop at her back, she had no way to escape so she slid her hands from around his neck and she used them instead to push at his chest, frantic suddenly for air and breathing space.

He froze for a heartbeat or two and then he stepped back, to her vast relief. They stared at each other and every sound in the kitchen seemed magnified. Her breathing seemed to come in ragged gulps and she had no idea how to react.

What must he think of her? She had responded to him like some sex-starved widow, desperate for a man's touch.

She found it small consolation that he looked thunderstruck, as if his lovely, elegant kitchen were suddenly teeming with bobcats.

She fumbled for words and came up empty. She had no experience in this sort of situation and didn't know the first thing to say to him. He let out a long breath and then raked a hand through his hair.

"Well. That was certainly…unexpected," he finally said.

Heat soaked her cheeks and she wanted to sink through his custom Italian tile floor. "Wasn't it?" she murmured, in as cool a voice as she could muster. She hurried to the sink and washed her hands, then picked up the mixing bowl and resumed stirring the ingredients for the flourless chocolate cake, grateful for any excuse not to have to look at him.

Still, she was intensely aware of him watching her out of those vibrant blue eyes. After a moment, he stepped closer and it was all she could do not to back up a pace.

"I should probably tell you I don't usually do that sort of thing."

She absolutely refused to allow her hands to shake, though it was taking every ounce of her concentration. "Kiss women?" She raised a skeptical eyebrow. "I'll admit, I'm not the most experienced rose in the garden but I find that a little hard to believe, judging by your proficiency at it."

He gave a surprised-sounding laugh but quickly sobered. "I meant I'm not in the habit of accosting employees."

She drew in a sharp breath at the stark reminder of the differences between them and all the reasons she should never have let him touch her. She felt foolish and remarkably naive—quite a feat for a woman who had been married for ten years and had four children.

"You didn't accost me. It was a simple kiss."

"Right."

If she found any solace in this entire situation, it was that Carson appeared as baffled and uneasy as she was by their heated embrace.

"I didn't mean for that to happen."

"Let's just forget it did, all right?"

He looked as if he wanted to argue but before he could form the words, her cell phone chirped out its cheery "Jingle Bells" ring tone. She fumbled in her pocket and for one humiliating moment, she couldn't pull it free, but she was finally able to grasp it and open it to talk.

She had barely said hello before Kip started babbling something about how his aunt had given him a new nutcracker for his collection only Hayden stole it and wouldn't give it back, claiming he was going to throw it in the woodstove.

"Make him stop, Mama! Make him *stop!*"

She sighed. On the one hand, she was grateful for the distraction from Carson. On the other, she truly hated mothering by phone.

"Calm down, honey. He's not going to throw anything into the woodstove. He's just teasing you because you get so upset."

"He's not. He said he was serious."

"Where's your aunt Terri?"

"In the garage talking to Uncle Paul. He's under the truck changing the oil. I got to help hand him a wrench."

"Good job. Let me talk to Hayden, okay?"

While she waited, she caught a glimpse of Carson still leaning against the counter watching her, his expression distant and unreadable.

A moment later, she heard Kip yelling down the hall, "Hayden, Mom wants to talk to you. You better give me back my nutcracker right now or you are in big trouble."

By the time she sorted through the situation and lectured Hayden on not teasing his younger siblings, Carson had left the kitchen.

She hadn't seen him go but she told herself she was relieved. The last thing she needed when she was so stressed about this job was for Carson to stand over her, making her forget her own name, not to mention whether she had added the turmeric to the soup.

She needed to concentrate on the meal she was preparing for dinner, not on the man who kissed her senseless.

Why had he kissed her?

That was the question that echoed through the kitchen the rest of the afternoon and haunted her long after she watched through the kitchen window as Carson and his guests left the ranch on horseback and headed up the trail toward the mountains through a light, powdery snowfall.

She knew why she had responded to him. What sane woman wouldn't? But she wasn't the kind of woman who inspired men like him to passionate embraces. She was a widow with four children, for heaven's sake, not some tight-bodied twenty-three-year-old socialite.

What did it matter? she finally asked herself. It was a fluke that would never be repeated. Somehow she was going to have to focus on the job at hand and not on that stunning, heart-stopping kiss.

She had only a few more meals to cook for him and his guests and then she would retreat to her family and leave Carson McRaven to rattle around alone here in his huge, gorgeous house.

Carson deliberately stayed out of the kitchen the rest of the day, though it was a challenge. With the strength of his fascination for Jenna, he might not have been able to do it if he hadn't spent most of the afternoon out of the house with the Hertzogs— or at least with Frederick and Dierk and the children. Antonia and Elle planned to stay at the house relaxing in the hot tub while Carson and the rest of his guests went riding.

He led them on horses up into the snow-covered mountains above the house, on a trail groomed by one of his men on the ranch's snowcat to make the going a little easier for the horses.

Mother Nature cooperated and provided a gorgeous afternoon, with only a light, feather-soft snowfall that made the entire scene look like something out of a watercolor painting.

He showed them the elk herd that wintered in one of the high pastures and the sixty-foot waterfall that was just beginning to ice over for the season.

Several hours later, they returned to the house tired and hungry just as twilight was settling over the valley and the lights of Jenna's house were beginning to sparkle in the snow.

The Christmas tree he and her boys had cut gleamed a welcome for them in the window and he was suddenly enormously grateful they had nagged him into it. Raven's Nest looked warm and inviting, exactly as he had always dreamed.

"Something certainly smells delicious," Frederick exclaimed as they walked into Raven's Nest after taking care of the horses.

Carson's stomach rumbled at the mingled scents emanating from the kitchen, of meats roasting and yeasty bread and something sweet and chocolaty.

"I am starving," Gregor said.

"We must clean up before we eat," his father said, his voice firm. "We all smell like the horses."

After thanking him for the ride and the tour of the ranch, the four of them headed up the stairs toward their guest quarters. Long after their voices faded, Carson stood in the hallway, fighting his inclination to follow those delectable smells to the even more delectable woman who had created them.

He didn't understand his fascination with her or the inexorable bonds that seemed to tug him toward her, even when he had been away from her for several hours. He only knew he needed to do everything in his power to fight his way free of them.

Despite her astonishingly heated response to his kiss, Jenna Wheeler was not the sort of woman who engaged in casual affairs and he wasn't interested in anything else.

No doubt she had cursed him all afternoon for kissing her. He had made a huge mistake, on many levels. On the most basic, she was an employee, at least temporarily. He had an ironclad rule *never* to fraternize with the many people who worked for him. He didn't like blurring the lines, complicating relationships. And his relationship with Jenna was nothing if not complicated.

More important, she was his neighbor and would be for a long time, especially since he had promised her he wouldn't have his people continue in their efforts to buy her house and land.

He would have dealings with her for years to come. Kissing her again, pursuing this desire that sizzled between them, would only make things awkward for both of them.

He had a sudden wish that things could go back to the way they had been several days ago, when he had found her boys tightrope walking on his fence. Something momentous had changed in that instant and he didn't like it. Not one damn bit.

With a sigh, he forced himself to walk up the stairs to shower and change for dinner. She would only be here a few more hours and then she would be going home for the night to her house and her noisy boys and the chaos of her life.

He only had to make it through dinner.

The task proved tougher than he had hoped. Jenna served the meal herself, dressed simply in black slacks and a white shirt. The clothes were different than the jeans she had worn earlier and he wondered if she had brought the change with her or if she had gone back to her house while he had been out riding.

He was painfully aware of her as she brought out course after course of divine food. A field-green salad with a unique spicy pecan vinaigrette, some kind of mushroom soup he thought he could eat every day for the rest of his life and be perfectly content, and the main course, a choice of either wild rainbow trout in a walnut crust or a savory filet mignon that melted in his mouth.

She didn't meet his gaze once throughout the meal, not even when she served dessert, which was either flourless chocolate cake or a pumpkin-swirled cheesecake.

"Mrs. Wheeler, you have a true gift with food," Antonia Hertzog said as Jenna set an elegantly garnished slice of cheesecake in front of her.

"Thank you," she murmured with a smile. She looked lovely and warm and he couldn't seem to look away from her.

He held his breath as she moved around the table to him and set a serving of the chocolate cake he had requested.

Her breasts barely brushed his shoulder as she set the plate down and he tensed every muscle, his mind unable to focus on anything but the memory of her softness against him when he had kissed her.

"Thank you," he said.

"You're welcome. Does anyone need anything else?"

He could come up with plenty of things but he decided it probably would be wise to keep his mind off of them.

"Do you have any Nutella?" Amalia whispered.

Jenna smiled at the girl, who had barely spoken to Carson though he had spent the entire afternoon with her. "I'm not completely sure, but I think I might have seen some in the kitchen. I'll go look for you."

She returned a moment later and set the jar down near Amalia, who gifted her with a brilliant smile. "Thank you." Her words were so low, Carson could barely hear them.

"No problem. Anytime you need more, it will be on the second shelf in the pantry, near the peanut butter."

"Thank you," the girl said again. Jenna smiled at her again and Carson had a ferocious wish that she would do the same to him sometime.

She turned to leave the room but he finally spoke, compelled in some ridiculous way to keep her a little closer, if only for a moment.

"Everything okay on the home front?" he asked. "No more nutcracker emergencies?"

She finally met his gaze and for just an instant, remembered heat flickered between them but she quickly looked away. "Not this evening. I took a moment to check on them a few hours ago and everyone was settling in for the night."

"Do you live nearby?" Dierk asked, watching Jenna with a male appreciation that made Carson bristle.

"Yes, actually. Just down the hill."

"The house with all the holiday lights?" Elle asked, just a miniscule dash of disdain in her voice.

Jenna either didn't hear it or she chose to ignore it. "That's the one. My family and I are Mr. McRaven's closest neighbors."

"Your home looks so very festive," Antonia said warmly, as if to make up for her daughter-in-law's chilly demeanor. "How many children do you have?"

Jenna smiled "Four."

"Four!" Antonia exclaimed. *"Ach der lieber!"*

"Yes. Three boys and a girl. My oldest is ten and my youngest, the only girl, is eighteen months."

"And their father? What does he do?" Elle asked. This time the supercilious tone was not quite as veiled.

Still, Jenna retained her calm, friendly demeanor. "He was a cattle rancher but he was killed in a ranch accident two years ago."

"Oh, you poor dear." Antonia reached out a hand and covered Jenna with hers. "I am so sorry."

"So am I," Jenna answered. "He was a good man and we all miss him very much."

She turned to leave but Frederick gestured to an extra chair against the wall. "You must have been on your feet all day to prepare such a wonderful feast. Why don't you stay and have dessert with us?"

For an instant Jenna looked taken aback by the offer but then she gave him a regretful smile. "Thank you very much for the kind offer, but I'm afraid I've got a few things to finish up in the kitchen for breakfast in the morning and then I really must return home to check on my children."

"Of course, of course," Frederick said.

She smiled at the group, though she still avoided Carson's gaze. "If anyone needs anything at all, please let me know," she said, then returned to the kitchen, leaving them to their dessert.

"A lovely woman," Frederick said after she was gone.

"Yes. She is." Carson couldn't shake the memory of her delicate features flushed and warm and desirable after their kiss.

"How lucky of you to have a chef living just down the hill, and such a lovely one at that," he said. "Has she worked for you long?"

He briefly thought about explaining the chain of events that had led Jenna to Raven's Nest but decided the truth didn't reflect well on him. Somehow he didn't think Frederick would appreciate the combination of bribery and blackmail it had taken to convince Jenna to cook for his house party. "Mrs. Wheeler doesn't really work for me. She is only here as a favor to me."

Antonia shook her head. "Imagine, four children and no one to help with them. She must be a truly remarkable woman."

Carson was beginning to agree, much to his vexation.

Jenna placed both hands in the small of her back and stretched, trying to work out some of the kinks from standing in a kitchen for fourteen hours.

Her shoulders felt weighted down with exhaustion but it wasn't an unpleasant sensation, more the comfortable tiredness that came from knowing the satisfaction of a job well done. She had worked hard but she found it gratifying that her efforts had been met with such obvious success.

She rotated her shoulders then shrugged off her fatigue to load another dish in the second dishwasher. The plan had been for Melina Parker to help her serve dinner and clean up afterward. But when she showed up earlier in the evening, her features had been tight and nearly gray with pain.

She had pretended everything was all right, apparently forgetting Jenna was raising three mischievous boys and had become quite an expert at worming information out of reticent subjects. After she applied her best interrogation skills on the other woman, Melina finally confessed she had been hit with a terrible migraine.

Though it meant a little extra work for her, Jenna couldn't let her suffer. She had ordered her to rest in a dark room until the headache passed.

It hadn't been too difficult. Really, for all her nerves earlier, the day had gone remarkably well. Her food had been well received and that was the important thing. All of the Hertzogs—with the exception of Elle, who looked as if she typically dined on celery stalks and lemon water—had been effusive in their praise and even Carson had eaten every bite of his filet mignon and a portion of trout, as well.

Not that she was neurotically checking or anything.

She sighed as she loaded another dish into the dishwasher. She had to get out of Raven's Nest before she became completely obsessed with the man.

One and a half more days—four more meals—and then she could return to her own family and Christmas and be able to sleep soundly in the knowledge that with the hefty fee Carson was paying her, she could pay off the small business loan she had taken out to start her catering business.

She had a few doubts about taking such a considerable sum from him but she had convinced herself she deserved it. Throwing together such a meal in only a few hours—especially only a few days before Christmas—was a considerable feat, one that deserved proper compensation.

Besides, he could afford it. The cost of his dishwasher alone would cover her business overhead for six months or more.

She definitely needed to stop thinking about Carson, she reminded herself. She'd made a vow to herself she would put the man out of her head, otherwise she would never get any sleep.

Forcing her mind to think instead about Christmas and all she still needed to do, she reached to return a serving tray onto a top shelf, then winced as the motion stretched the already-tight muscle where her neck met her shoulder. She rubbed at it, trying to work out the knot to no avail.

While she massaged at the ache, she paused to look out the window at the glowing lights of town, just barely visible at the mouth of Cold Creek Canyon.

Carson truly did have a lovely view here, in every direction, really. The soaring western slope of the Tetons was just visible above the smaller mountains around Pine Gulch and from here, Cold Creek glowed silver in the moonlight.

And the house itself was gorgeous, she had to admit, though a bit on the cold side. She would have liked to see a little more life in it. Some children's artwork—and handprints—on the refrigerator, a few toys scattered on the floor, perhaps a school backpack hanging on one of those empty hooks by the door.

The house needed a little life and warmth. Maybe Carson did too, she thought, then chided herself for letting her thoughts wander back to him.

"You look like you could use a soak in the hot tub."

At the deep voice, she whirled around to find the man who had occupied far too many of her thoughts standing in the doorway, looking ruggedly masculine in the tan slacks and white shirt he had worn to dinner.

To her dismay, despite the lecture she had given herself all evening, her heart started to accelerate and for a moment she could do nothing but stare at him.

Chapter Nine

"I didn't hear you come in."

"You looked as if you were lost in thought. And like a woman who has been on her feet all day."

He took a step into the kitchen and she wondered how it was possible for the massive room to suddenly feel so tight and claustrophobic.

"I was just thinking what a lovely view you have from here. I've been wondering all day why Joe's great-grandfather didn't place his house in exactly this spot. I suppose it was logical in those days to build the homestead close to the creek where they drew their water, but up here makes far more sense from a purely aesthetic point of view."

"I suppose the early Pine Gulch settlers had a few more things on their mind than aesthetics. Survival probably carried a little more weight with them."

"You're probably right."

She knew exactly what it was like to exist purely in survival mode. She had done just that in the terrible months after Joe's death, when she had been fighting so desperately to keep the ranch afloat while she was pregnant and grieving and trying to be strong for her three little boys who had missed their father so much.

But time moved on. She moved on. Day by day, that bleak, wintry world had given way to sunshine. Jolie's birth had been a big part of that. Selling the ranch had helped as well, she acknowledged, despite how much she had agonized about the decision.

"Anyway," Carson said, "you are more than welcome to use the pool or the Jacuzzi anytime. I know you said at dinner you needed to get home to your kids tonight but if you'd like to come early in the morning, please feel free, or even when we leave for the ski resort after breakfast."

She tried to picture herself enjoying a soak in that luxurious indoor hot tub overlooking the valley. It was a lovely image right now with every muscle in her body aching, but she knew she would never be able to bring herself to get quite *that* comfortable in Carson's house.

"Thank you. But right now, all I want is a hot shower and my bed."

For just an instant, something bright and glittery sparked in his eyes and her insides gave a long, slow roll. She drew in a breath and pushed away the reaction, frustrated at her weakness when it came to him.

"Is everything all set for tomorrow?" he asked. "Do you need anything else?"

"I think I'll be fine. According to the menu your assistant sent me, breakfast in the morning was to be macadamia banana pancakes with orange butter. I'm also adding a smoked salmon and asparagus frittata. Is that still acceptable?"

"You're making my mouth water just thinking about it, even though I'm full from the wonderful dinner."

"I thought you all might need more protein before you go skiing. I know it always used to help me to eat a high-protein breakfast before I hit the slopes."

"You ski?"

"I used to snowboard in college, if you can believe that."

He stared at her and she had to laugh. "Should I be insulted that you look so astonished? Do you think I'm too old and settled to be a snowboarder?"

"No. I was just trying to wrap my head around it. You're just full of surprises, aren't you?"

What did he mean by that? She flushed, remembering how she had responded to his unexpected kiss.

"I wasn't a bad boarder, either. It's been a while, though. We used to take the boys to Jackson but I haven't had much time the last few years."

"Why don't you bring the boys and come with us tomorrow?"

Now it was her turn to stare and she forgot about being tired. "Now who's full of surprises? You're inviting my energetic boys to spend the day snowboarding with the international guests whose European business interests you're trying to purchase? Are you completely insane?"

"I'm beginning to think so," he murmured. Or at least she *thought* that's what he said but he spoke too low for her to completely understand.

"Well, thank you for the invitation," she said, "but I'm going to have to pass, though Hayden would wring my neck if he knew. He's been bothering me since the first snowfall to take him."

"Why don't you, then?"

She shook her head. "Do you have any idea of the logistics that would be involved? I don't think any of their snowsuits still fit, for one thing. They're getting new ones for Christmas but that's still four days away. And beyond that, if my boys and I go off having a grand time at the ski resort with the Hertzogs, how, exactly, do you expect me to prepare your dinner tomorrow night?"

"We could figure something out."

"No. Thank you, but no. That's one of the things on our list for Christmas vacation. You go and have a good time with your guests and I'll stay here and make sure you have something edible at the end of the day."

"If you change your mind, let me know."

She nodded, though, of course, she wouldn't. In her preoccupation with his unexpected invitation, she hadn't paid any mind to what he was doing while they discussed snowboarding but now she realized while she was arguing with him, he had stepped to the sink and started drying and putting away dishes.

"Hey, stop right now," she said suddenly.

He blinked at her. "Stop what?"

"Cleaning up! You don't have to do that. You're paying me a ridiculously obscene amount to take care of those little details."

"I don't mind. I've washed plenty of dishes in my day."

She blinked. "You? The CEO of McRaven Enterprises?"

He gave a rough-sounding laugh. "Fifteen years ago McRaven Enterprises didn't exist. I was CEO of exactly nothing."

"Fifteen years? You've done amazing things in that short amount of time."

While she had been busy having babies, he had been making his fortune. She supposed that might depress some women but she wouldn't have traded her life for anything, even with all the pain and sorrow on the road of her life's journey.

"I had a few breaks when I was first starting out," he said. "Things have snowballed from there. I've been really extraordinarily lucky."

That wasn't true, she knew. Before she would even consider selling him the ranch, she had researched all she could about him. She knew his reputation for taking faltering or stagnating tech businesses and turning them around.

"You don't have to use false modesty with me, Carson. Everything I've read about you says you're brilliant, that you have almost single-handedly made McRaven Enterprises a force to be reckoned with."

He looked uncomfortable with her praise, almost embarrassed, something she never would have expected. She found it startling and more than a little appealing.

"Not bad for a guy who had to take the GED to get a high-school diploma and barely made it through college taking night classes," he said lightly, with far more self-deprecation than she would have ever imagined.

He reached into the refrigerator for a Perrier and twisted the cap and she had the feeling the action was purely to cover his discomfort from talking about himself.

She didn't remember reading about his early beginnings in any of the articles she had seen about him. Such a humble background made his current success all the more remarkable and clearly reflected that he was a man of focus and determination, something she had already figured out for herself.

She knew she should go home. She had a million things to do, though she also knew from a quick phone call to her niece, Erin, that all the children were sound asleep. Still, she felt strangely content in such quiet conversation with him and she was suddenly reluctant to end it.

"You never married?"

He took a long sip of water. When he lowered the bottle, she saw a change in his expression, as if something dark and sad had slid across it. His mouth compressed into a tight line.

"I was married once. A long time ago."

He spoke reluctantly, as if he didn't share that information with many people, and she almost regretted asking him.

"How long is a long time?" she asked.

"Well, I was barely eighteen. I'm thirty-six now. I guess you can do the math."

She didn't remember reading anything about a marriage or a divorce in any of the articles she had found about him but she supposed if the event had been so long ago, he had probably preferred to keep the information private.

Maybe he wasn't divorced. She pushed the thought away. She would have known when she sold him the ranch if he had a wife hanging around somewhere. The sale documents had been complicated and detailed and surely that information would have come to light.

"They say young marriages have a rougher road. I suppose that must be true."

He sipped at his water again with a faraway look. "It wasn't easy, by any means. Suzanna was only seventeen and we were young and naive and thought we could handle anything."

"Most teenagers do."

That made him smile, though it didn't quite reach his eyes. "Right. Well, both of us were escaping rough home lives and had some sort of idealistic plan to rescue each other, I guess."

He shrugged. "I'm not sure we ever really intended to marry. I don't know that we would have if Suzanna hadn't discovered she was pregnant."

Pregnant? He had a child somewhere?

"That sort of changed everything. We decided we would try to hold things together and try to build a future together, so we scraped together enough for a marriage license and got married at a justice of the peace. I worked construction in the day and washed dishes at night so we could afford an armpit of an apartment in Oakland."

He said he and his wife had both been escaping bad home lives. She wondered what sort of misery he had endured and was grateful again for her own parents who had provided her with nothing but love through her childhood.

"What happened with your marriage?" she asked, though she was almost afraid to hear the answer. Somehow she sensed by his suddenly stark expression that it had a grim ending.

He was quiet for several moments. The only sound in the kitchen was the soft tick of the clock. She thought perhaps he wasn't going to answer and was just about to apologize for her rude prying when he let out a heavy breath. "She died in childbirth, along with our son."

Oh, dear heaven. She never would have expected that answer.

Jenna gazed at him as sadness soaked through her. He had lost a wife and a child who never had a chance at life.

She felt as if everything she thought she had known about Carson had just been tossed in a hundred directions.

All this time she had thought him cold, hard, distant. Arrogant, even. He was so reserved with her children—and even with the Hertzog children—but now she wondered if he used that stoic, even stony, demeanor as a mask.

Nothing she said could ease his heartache but she knew first-hand how very much simple condolences could mean to a grieving heart.

"I'm sorry, Carson. So very sorry."

Her low words seemed to echo through the quiet kitchen, reaching deep inside him to a raw wound he thought had healed long ago.

Why the hell was he telling her this? He never talked about Suz and their baby. Never. There wasn't another soul on earth who knew this part of his past, of the guilt and pain that had been his constant companions for so long after her death.

He had been so alone, so angry. Just a stupid, powerless punk, bitter at the world and especially at the substandard hospital's emergency room that had delayed admitting her because they were a poor teenage couple without health insurance, and at the incompetent doctors who hadn't diagnosed her toxemia in time to save either of them.

Mostly he had been consumed with guilt. He had vowed to love and cherish and take care of Suz and their baby and he had screwed up.

He still carried that guilt inside him like an anchor, though he had become so accustomed to it after all these years that it just seemed a part of him now.

He knew it had been his fault she died. If he had done a better job providing for them, it wouldn't have happened. Early in her pregnancy he had taken a construction job with health insurance but had ended up walking out because of the callous way the company treated its workers.

She had wanted to apply for government assistance, as her mother and sisters and everyone else in the inner-city projects where she had grown up had done. But Carson's prickly pride wouldn't allow it. He had promised her he would find another position with insurance before she had the baby, but times had been tough and he had failed. And because of his pride and stupid convictions, his wife and son had died.

He could never forgive himself for that.

He had vowed as he stood over the two side-by-side graves that he would never allow anyone else to depend on him. He couldn't be counted on, nor could he count on anyone else. His childhood had taught him that.

He had worked hard to graduate from college in three years by taking a double load of classes. He had used the small malpractice settlement from the hospital to invest in his first company, a failing Silicon Valley software start-up with a winning product but poor management. He had turned it around in eighteen months then bought another company and another and had been doing it ever since.

Every McRaven company provided extensive health-care programs for its employees, especially prenatal care. It was a primary part of the business model.

None of the success he found would ever ease the guilt over those two lives that had depended on him.

"What was his name?"

He blinked away the past and realized Jenna was watching him closely, her features soft with sympathy.

"Your son," she said when he didn't answer. "What did you name him?"

"Suzanna picked out Henry James. She'd always loved the author—and the name—so that's what I stuck with."

He didn't think about his son as often as he thought of his young wife. He had loved the idea of having a child as much as it had terrified him, but mostly he had been happy because Suzanna had been happy. She glowed with joy and hope at the idea of bringing new life into the world—a minor miracle itself, since her upbringing in deep poverty and despair would have left most women cynical about the future.

Henry James McRaven would have been graduating from high school this year. It was a stunning realization.

"I'm sorry," Jenna said again. She laid a hand on his arm with a comforting kind of gesture that seemed a sweet balm to the aching corner inside him.

"It seems like another lifetime ago. I was a different person."

"But it's one of the things that shaped the man you've become, isn't it?"

"Yes. Without question."

It had been a terrible time in his life, one he wouldn't wish on anyone, but those years had defined everything that came after.

If Suzanna and Henry had lived, he didn't know what course his life would have taken. He certainly wouldn't have been so driven to prove something to the cold, heartless bitch he called fate.

He studied Jenna, this woman who had somehow managed to reach through his careful barriers and tug out memories and experiences he had always believed he preferred to keep close inside him.

"So what events in your past helped shape the woman you've become?"

She leaned against the marble work island, her head tilted as she appeared to consider his words. "I'm still very much a work in progress."

"Aren't we all?"

A warm intimacy surrounded them in the quiet kitchen. That connection he had been fighting all day seemed to tighten between them.

He should leave right now, before this thing between them grew even stronger. He knew it was the wise course—and he was a man who prided himself on his prudence. But he couldn't seem to make himself move from this spot. He wanted to know about her, he discovered.

"If you had to pick the top three events that shaped you, what would make the list?" he asked impulsively.

She made a face. "No fair asking me to have a coherent thought after I've been on my feet since seven o'clock," she protested. "Anyway, I don't know if I could narrow it down to three."

"Try."

She paused for a moment, her forehead furrowed in concentration. "Well, I suppose off the top of my head—and purely in chronological order—the first thing would have to be my parents' death in a car accident when I was sixteen. My brother Paul had just turned twenty-one and he became legal guardian to me. I was a sixteen-year-old girl who thought she was invincible and that was the first time I realized the precariousness, the fragility, of life."

"That's one."

Her features grew pensive. "Of course, I would have to include falling in love with Joe the summer before I graduated from college, and then marrying him and moving home to Pine Gulch to stay for good. Hand in hand with that would have to be the births of each of our beautiful children. Those four wise little souls shaped me more than anything else."

She grew quiet, her eyes shadowed. "Then my world and my children's was forever changed two years ago on October 15 when a tractor rolled over on the man I thought I would spend the rest of my life with, crushing our future together. I guess that's three."

A few days ago, he would have thought he had little in common with a woman like Jenna Wheeler. But the pain in her eyes was only too familiar. For a long time after Suzanna's death, he had seen it gazing back at him in the mirror.

"It sucks, doesn't it?" he said.

She was speechless for a moment then she laughed, a low, surprised sound that somehow lifted his spirits.

NO POSTAGE
NECESSARY
IF MAILED
IN THE
UNITED STATES

BUSINESS REPLY MAIL
FIRST-CLASS MAIL   PERMIT NO. 717   BUFFALO, NY

POSTAGE WILL BE PAID BY ADDRESSEE

SILHOUETTE READER SERVICE
3010 WALDEN AVE
PO BOX 1867
BUFFALO NY 14240-9952

Do You Have the LUCKY KEY?

PLAY THE Lucky Key Game

and you can get

FREE BOOKS and FREE GIFTS!

Scratch the gold areas with a coin. Then check below to see the books and gifts you can get!

YES! I have scratched off the gold areas. Please send me the **2 FREE BOOKS** and **2 FREE GIFTS**, worth about $10, for which I qualify. I understand I am under no obligation to purchase any books, as explained on the back of this card.

335 SDL EVL5   235 SDL EVQH

FIRST NAME   LAST NAME

ADDRESS

APT.#   CITY

STATE/ PROV.   ZIP/POSTAL CODE

www.eHarlequin.com

2 free books plus 2 free gifts   1 free book

2 free books   Try Again!

"It really does. That's the perfect word for it."

He wanted to kiss her again. He had spent all day telling himself why that would be a grievous mistake, but right now none of those reasons seemed very important. She was soft and warm and eminently desirable here in the quiet of his kitchen.

He leaned forward slightly and he could smell her again, that strangely seductive scent of vanilla and cinnamon.

Her gaze met his and in those glittery green depths he saw the same spark of awareness that sizzled through him, the same subtle yearning.

She caught her breath and leaned toward him slightly, her weight canted onto her toes.

His nerves tightened with anticipation and he moved to close the last few inches between them.

At the very last second, just when his mouth would have covered hers, she turned her head and took a jerky step backward.

"Please don't, Carson. Not again." She let out a shaky breath and he saw her hands were trembling.

Frustration burned through him. She had been ready for his kiss, had parted her lips in clear invitation. He knew he hadn't imagined it. "Why not?"

"Because it's completely unfair!" Her voice was heated. "I have no defenses against a man like you."

"What the hell is that supposed to mean?"

She drew her hands to her suddenly rosy cheeks, then dropped them as if the heat there burned her fingers. "I have dated one man seriously in my life and I married him a year later. I'm not the sort of sophisticated socialite who can do the casual affair thing. I'm just not."

"What makes you think that's what I want?"

She gave him an impatient look. "You will break my heart, Carson. I'm sure you won't mean to but you'll do it anyway because that's the kind of man you are."

Her words shouldn't have the power to hurt him but they

sliced him open anyway. "How do you know what kind of man I am?"

Her laugh sounded sharply discordant after the warm intimacy they had just shared. "Look at you. You're like something out of a movie. Gorgeous, rich, successful. I'm the mother of four children, hanging by my fingernails on the ledge of a wild, turbulent world. You will chew me up and spit me out and there will be absolutely nothing I can do about it. When whatever this is is out of your system, I will be left here living just down the hill from Raven's Nest, forced to see your house out my window and remember."

"It doesn't have to be that way."

"You're right. You're absolutely right. We can go back to the place we were before you…before you kissed me this afternoon. I had hoped we were on our way to being, if not friends, at least friendly."

"That's what you want? A friend?"

"Right now I want to go home to my children. I've been away too long. I'll be back first thing in the morning for breakfast."

He wanted to argue with her. To tell her he had never known anything like his attraction to her. But how could he possibly refute what he knew was absolute truth?

"That snow has made everything slick. Be careful."

Her smile was rueful and, he thought, a little sad. "What do you think the last five minutes was all about?"

Before he could answer, she grabbed her scarf and coat off the hook by the back door and headed out into the snow.

A few moments later, he watched her van's headlights cut through the night as she headed down the drive toward her house.

She was right. Somehow they needed to step back a bit. What other option was there? She wasn't interested in anything casual and he would never allow anything else. As soon as Christmas was over, he would be heading back to California, to his deals and his penthouse and the life he had carved out for himself, as empty and cold as that suddenly seemed.

Chapter Ten

"Mom, Hayden won't move so we can see. Make him cut it out!"

Jenna closed her eyes and whispered a quick, fervent prayer for patience. She looked toward the closed kitchen door that led to the rest of the house and then back toward the small couch and love seat where her boys were sitting by the fireplace in their pajamas.

"Come on, guys. Hayden, quit teasing your brothers. You promised. I just need you all to sit quietly and watch Rudolph for a while, okay? And then Aunt Terri will be here to take you back to the house."

"This is a baby show," Hayden grumbled.

"What are you talking about? This is your favorite show!"

"No way. It's totally stupid."

She glared at her oldest. He was such a leader to the other boys. If they picked up his lead and refused to watch the DVD she had brought, she just might have a mutiny on her hands, which was the absolute last thing she needed when she still had a hundred things to do before breakfast in an hour.

When had her oldest son become too old to enjoy one of the classic Christmas specials? It was a tough age for a boy, she knew. He was ten and struggling to decide if he still wanted to be a boy or a preadolescent. Since his father's death she had watched him as he tried to grow up faster than she thought he should.

She had desperately tried to avoid exactly this scenario—having to bring the children with her to Raven's Nest while she prepared breakfast for Carson and his guests. She thought she had everything arranged and had planned to have her niece, Erin, sleep over so she could spend the morning with the children.

But when she returned to her house the night before, after that awkward encounter with Carson, Erin had apologetically informed her she forgot she had promised to cover a friend's paper route and had to be home to take care of it.

She had hoped to be finished before Jenna had to leave for Raven's Nest but Terri had called her and said the route was taking longer than they planned because of the snow. They expected to be done in the next hour.

She had to keep her fingers crossed and hope the holiday magic of Rudolph and his friends would keep the children preoccupied enough that they wouldn't start ripping apart Carson's house.

If not for Hayden, it just might work. Jolie was still sound asleep in one corner of the couch and the other two boys were at least moderately interested, though she could see the indecision in their eyes. If Hayden called it a baby show, neither Drew nor Kip would be caught dead watching it.

She considered her maternal grab bag of manipulation techniques and decided the fine art of diversion was a proven winner. "If you don't want to watch the show, why don't you come and help me?"

He opened his mouth to protest but then a crafty light entered his green eyes. "Will you pay me as much as you're paying Erin to sit with us? She says she's making a ton."

She smiled. "I guess that depends on how much help you are. While I crack the eggs for the frittata, why don't you come and peel these oranges so we can squeeze them for juice?"

He looked less than thrilled but apparently he decided the possibility of a little coin was more exciting than watching a baby show with his brothers.

It was actually quite enjoyable working beside him while the DVD played quietly in the background. She had discovered these small moments working one-on-one with her children provided an invaluable opportunity for conversation she would normally miss. With four children, she sometimes felt stretched thin when all of them were talking to her at once. She had learned to cherish any opportunity to interact with them individually—even when she was knee-deep in work making a gourmet breakfast for seven people.

For twenty minutes, she and Hayden talked about his favorite subject right now, football, and his favorite team, the Denver Broncos. The time flew past as they talked about passing percentages and wild card play-off slots and player trades. They talked about school and about his friends and his plans for the rest of Christmas vacation.

The time flew past and before she knew it, a quick check of the clock told her it was 7:10 a.m. and Carson's guests were expecting breakfast in twenty minutes.

She just might make it, she thought as she poured the freshly squeezed juice into a crystal pitcher.

The door to the kitchen suddenly opened and her ridiculous heart skipped a beat when Carson appeared in Levi's and an earth-toned sweater. His dark hair was damp and he was freshly shaved and all she could think about for one crazy moment was the stunning heat they had shared the day before.

"Mom, the orange juice is spilling!" Hayden exclaimed.

She looked down and realized she had just wasted a good cup or more of his hard work by letting the pitcher overflow. Juice dripped all over the countertop in a sticky orange mess.

She flushed and reached for the roll of paper towels. "Sorry," she muttered.

"Is the coffee ready?" Carson asked.

"It should be." She couldn't quite bring herself to meet his gaze, though she was painfully aware of him.

"Smells good in here."

She suddenly remembered the scent of him, masculine and sexy, and ordered herself to stop. She would never stop blushing if she couldn't manage to focus on breakfast.

"I was still shooting for seven-thirty for everything to be ready." She forced her voice to be brisk and professional as she finished cleaning up the orange juice and turned her attention to the final thing on her list, the batch of currant muffins she had added to the menu at the last minute. "Does that time still work for you and your guests?"

"Everybody seems to be stirring. Frederick was getting in a swim a minute ago but he looked like he was just ready to get out. We were trying to head to the slopes in Jackson by eight-thirty."

"I love to snowboard," Hayden announced. "My dad used to take me before he died. I'm saving up to buy a new snowboard and I almost have enough."

That was the first she had heard of that particular plan. Last she knew, Hayden was saving to go to a football camp at Idaho State in the summer.

"You've got helpers this morning."

She gave Carson a quick look, trying to gauge his reaction to her children's presence, but he only looked impassive and rather distant. "Yes. I didn't have a choice. If you've got a problem with it, I'm more than willing to let you make your own currant muffins."

He raised an eyebrow. "Did I say I had a problem with it? I was simply making an observation."

She hadn't meant to sound so defensive or confrontational and she worked to moderate her tone.

"My niece is supposed to be tending them for me this morning but something came up and she can't get here for another—" she glanced at the omnipresent clock on the river-rock fireplace "—fifteen minutes. They have promised they'd be on their best behavior until then and so far they've been great. We've been here nearly an hour and you didn't even know they were here, did you?"

"I didn't hear a sound," he assured her as he moved to the coffeemaker and pulled a mug out of the cupboard above it.

He poured a cup but before he could take a sip, Jenna heard a squeaking kind of sound and looked down to see Jolie had awakened while she had been talking to Carson.

Her daughter stood next to her in her red footie pajamas, hanging on to Jenna's pant leg with one hand as she rubbed her bleary eyes.

"Hi, baby."

"Mama. Up."

Jenna was elbow-deep in muffin batter. She looked helplessly down at her daughter. "Oh, honey, I can't pick you up right now. Give me a minute, okay?"

"Mama! Up!" Jolie's voice rose in pitch and intensity and her eyes started to brim with tears. She was such a cuddler when she just woke up and she wasn't happy unless she'd been held for a few moments until she was ready to start the day.

"Do you want me to get her?" Hayden didn't bother to mask the reluctance in his voice.

"No. Want Mama!" Jolie had that stubborn set to her jaw that Jenna recognized only too well, since she shared it with each of her three older brothers. She was just trying to figure out how she could possibly finish the muffins with one hand while holding her daughter in the other when Carson moved toward them.

"Here. Let me try."

She stared in shock as Carson set down his coffee mug and scooped Jolie into his arms. Jenna waited for her daughter's tantrum after finding herself confronted with a stranger. Though her eyes widened and she looked startled, she didn't let out the wail Jenna had expected.

"Um, thanks," she murmured, aware of a weird tightness in her chest as she saw him holding her little girl.

After another moment, Jolie apparently decided she didn't mind her new position.

"Hi," she beamed after a moment, putting out her most adorable vibe.

Now that he had offered to help, Carson looked as if he didn't quite know what to do next with the squirming bundle of toddler. "Hi, yourself."

Jolie patted his cheek. "Nice," she declared.

Jenna knew she should be finishing breakfast but she couldn't seem to look away from their interaction. She saw Carson blink a little at that, then he smiled back at Jolie, a heartbreak of a smile that made her forget everything she was doing.

"Thanks," he answered. "You're pretty nice, too."

Oh, she was a goner.

Jenna could handle a kiss that curled her toes. She could protect herself against shared confidences in the quiet of a kitchen while a soft snowfall drifted down outside.

But she had absolutely no way to shield her heart from a man who could look so completely masculine and sexy—and so adorably flummoxed—holding one of her babies.

Talk about your crazy impulses.

He should have just turned around and walked out of the kitchen the moment this terrifying little creature wandered over to her mother, all big-eyed and soft and sleepy.

He didn't know the first thing about kids, especially girl kids. Jenna's older boys were one thing. They could at least carry on a basic conversation and were somewhat capable of rational thought. At least he assumed as much.

The little girl, though. She was something else entirely.

Her hair was messy, with blond curls sticking in every direction, and she just watched him out of those big, dark-lashed green eyes that were so much like her mother's.

Just what was he supposed to do with her? She babbled something incomprehensible to him. He tried to interpret it so he could answer but she didn't appear to need a response. She just giggled and continued babbling along.

Not sure what to do, he just pretended to follow her gibberish and occasionally made a benign comment as if he understood her.

"Is that right?" he said, which mostly just sent her off into more giggles.

Somewhere in the middle of the nonsensical conversation Carson forgot about feeling foolish. He forgot about his guests and about Jenna watching him out of those wary eyes while she fixed breakfast and about the call to Currianne he was hoping to find time to squeeze in before they left for the Jackson Hole ski slopes.

All he could focus on was this curly-haired girl with the huge eyes and wide, toothy smile.

He carried her around the kitchen, pointing out different things to her that he had never paid much attention to. The colorful tile backsplash behind the oven, the sprayer on the sink faucet, the ice maker on the refrigerator. She seemed to find everything fascinating as she jabbered at him.

By the time Jenna opened the oven door several moments later and slid in the pan of muffins, little Jolie Wheeler had completely stolen his heart.

"She doesn't usually take to anyone like that, especially men," Jenna said and he wondered if he ought to be insulted by her baffled surprise. "She's just not used to them, I guess, since she really only has interaction with her uncle Paul. I really thought she would be crying by now."

"I guess that just proves not all females run away from me in a panic."

She quickly looked at her boys, who were too busy watching the end of a holiday show to pay them any attention. When she shifted her gaze back to him, she was glaring, her expression clearly conveying that she thought him ill-mannered to mention the day before.

"I didn't run away," she muttered.

"What would you call it?" he asked, while Jolie was occupied suddenly banging a wooden spoon on the countertop.

"Mom, we can't hear the song!" Drew complained and Jenna swiftly slid a silicone cutting board across the countertop to muffle the banging.

"Using a little common sense."

He had promised himself after a sleepless night that he wouldn't push her, that he would try his best to forget his attraction to her. He was a little astonished that he was finding that so difficult to do this morning, especially with all four of her children right there with them.

She looked fresh and lovely this morning, with all her blond hair tightly contained in a French braid. She hardly looked old enough to be the mother of this little one in his arms, forget about three active boys.

"Thanks for your help with her, but you really can give her to one of her brothers. They're all a big help with her."

"She's fine for now, aren't you, bug?"

The girl gave him that wide smile again. "Jolie bug."

He grinned and looked up to find Jenna gazing at his mouth again.

His insides clenched and he suddenly wanted to shove all the children out of the kitchen and take their mother in his arms. He stared at her for a long moment that was only broken by a knock on the back door off the kitchen.

Jenna blinked a few times and he watched her swallow. Then she set down her spoon and hurried to answer the door.

A woman and a teenage girl who looked about fifteen stood in the doorway.

"Sorry we're so late, Aunt Jenna. The papers were delivered to us late and they were huge and took us a long time to roll."

"Lots of last-minute Christmas ads," the woman added as she walked into the room. "So this is the castle kitchen. Swank."

"And the lord of the manor," Jenna muttered, gesturing toward Carson.

He stepped forward to greet them and he saw surprise flicker in the older woman's eyes when she saw the little pajama-clad bundle in his arms.

"Hi." He smiled. "Welcome to Raven's Nest."

"Carson McRaven, this is my sister-in-law, Terri Patterson, and my niece, Erin. Without their help you would be eating dry cereal and peanut butter sandwiches right now."

The woman gave him a guarded look. "Hello," she answered.

Jolie wasn't nearly as restrained. "Auntie!" she exclaimed and clapped her hands in delight.

"Hi, pretty girl." She held out her hands and Jolie lunged into them.

His arms felt curiously bereft without the little girl in them and he wasn't quite sure what to do with them.

Jenna watched Carson shove his hands into the back pockets of his jeans and she tried to decipher his odd expression.

On a different man, she might have thought him hesitant to relinquish the toddler. But that certainly couldn't be true, she decided. The sooner Terri and Erin took the kids out of his hair, the better Carson would probably like it.

"Thanks again for watching the boys today," Jenna said to Erin. "I know you have a million things to do before you leave for the cruise on Christmas Eve."

"I don't have anything else to do. I'm already packed," Erin assured her with a grin. "I have been for two weeks. And with what you're paying me, I'll have even more money to spend in the duty-free stores onboard the ship."

She smiled. Erin was a world-class shopper and often lamented the tragic fact that Pine Gulch didn't have its own mall.

"I should be back at the house in a few hours and then I don't have to be back at Raven's Nest until early afternoon to start the dinner prep."

"No problem," Erin assured her. "Come on, you guys. We can watch the rest of the show at your house."

"This TV is bigger," Kip complained.

"Sorry, you're just going to have to slum it at home," Erin told him with a grin.

As she kissed each of her children goodbye, Jenna was aware of Carson still standing in the kitchen watching out of those blue eyes that seemed to miss nothing.

The next few moments were a flurry of activity—finding coats, grabbing the DVD, ushering everyone out the door.

"Be careful, the steps are a little icy." Jenna offered one last warning, then closed the door behind her family.

Carson was still there, one hip leaning against the kitchen counter. He had picked up his coffee mug again and he sipped at the contents, which must surely be lukewarm by now.

"This really has been a hassle for you to help me, hasn't it?" he said. "I don't know if I fully realized the logistics of it all until right now, watching you herd them all out the door."

"Yes," she said without equivocating. "But you're paying me extraordinarily well to compensate for any inconvenience."

His mouth compressed a little. "That still doesn't make it any easier for you. I suppose you're glad you're only committed to a few more meals. Dinner tonight and then breakfast in the morning and then everything can return to normal."

"Right," she murmured, though she couldn't quite figure out why that prospect should depress her.

Chapter Eleven

She only saw Carson briefly again before he and his guests left for skiing, when she replenished the buffet-style breakfast dishes she had prepared into the dining room.

He didn't look up at her from his spot at the dining table, where he seemed to be engrossed in conversation with the beautifully sophisticated Elle.

She was grateful, she told herself. She didn't need another encounter with him to upset her equilibrium. She was already wasting entirely too much of her time thinking about the man.

They all left shortly after breakfast and the huge rambling house seemed to echo in their absence.

She cleared the breakfast dishes and did as much of the prep work for dinner as she could then stood for a moment in the kitchen.

She had Raven's Nest to herself, and while she knew she needed to return to her children quickly, she couldn't resist taking a moment to look around, as she had really only seen the kitchen and dining area.

She walked slowly through the great room, with its massive river-rock fireplace soaring two stories high and the Christmas tree Carson had cut with her boys.

Opposite the great room was the indoor pool and Jacuzzi, which had equally impressive two-story windows overlooking the ranch.

Like the kitchen, no detail had been spared in the house, from the carved interior doors to the remote controlled window shades.

She couldn't deny it was elegant, with graceful lines and comfortable furnishings. She believed they called the decor mountain chic. Sure, a designer might use homespun-looking fabric for the curtains but it no doubt cost a couple hundred dollars a yard.

Even the Christmas tree looked off, somehow. Melina Parker told her Carson had brought in a team of designers to decorate it. Perhaps that was why something about it didn't look quite right. It was beautiful, but perhaps too polished. Or maybe it was the complete dearth of presents underneath it, a sight that sent a weird pang through her heart.

She wandered up the stairs, the railing polished and cool beneath her fingers. At the top of the stairs, she opened a door and realized with some chagrin that this must be the master bedroom.

The room was luxuriously appointed, with its own rock fireplace, a sitting area, a wide wall of windows overlooking her house and the valley and a huge four-poster log bed.

It was lavish and comfortable, she had to admit. But there were no personal mementos in sight. No photographs, no knick-knacks, nothing to show the individual personality of the man who lived here.

She found it terribly sad, though perhaps his house in San Francisco was filled with those sorts of accoutrements. Somehow she doubted it. He struck her as a man who had created a self-contained life for himself, one without distractions or unnecessary details.

She trailed a hand over the thick designer comforter on the bed, then jerked herself out of her reverie and ordered herself to stop this fascination with the man and go back to where she belonged.

Christmas was three days away and heaven knows, she still had a million items on her to-do list. She certainly had things she ought to be worried about other than Carson McRaven. The man could buy and sell whatever he wanted and she was fairly certain he would not appreciate her sympathy.

Dinner on his guests' last night was a rousing success, even more spectacular than the night before.

Jenna outdid herself with a choice of roast wild turkey or pork medallions so flavorful he was certain he had never tasted anything so delicious. In addition to creamy mashed potatoes and a fresh green salad with roasted pecans, she provided three kinds of dessert—mocha crème brûlée, cherry brownies with homemade vanilla ice cream and key lime pie.

She had a definite gift, he would give her that much. Most of the time he didn't even think about what he was eating, but Jenna's food was too memorable to ignore.

She could find a job as a personal chef anywhere. If not for the weird currents between them, he would offer her a full-time position at Raven's Nest. As a chef, she was creative and innovative and took risks that still somehow worked.

And amazingly, she presented the entire meal without meeting his gaze one single time.

Melina actually served most of the meal but Jenna came in a few times, once to bring the Nutella out to Amalia and once to answer a question from Antonia about an ingredient in the soup that turned out to be saffron.

Both times, she acted as if Carson didn't exist. So much for the friendship she claimed she wanted with him, though he refused to wallow in the self-pity that seemed, oddly, to hover at the edges of his consciousness.

It had been a strange day all the way around. Though the snow had been light and perfect and the skiing hard and aggressive, he had felt off his stride. He blamed it on the two Wheeler females. He couldn't seem to get Jenna out of his head. The sweet, heady taste of her, those soft, womanly curves, the unexpected heat of her response.

He didn't know when a simple kiss had affected him so profoundly.

But he also blamed some of his distraction on a twenty-five-pound little sprite with curly blonde hair and her mother's green eyes. He didn't like the tug in the vicinity of his heart whenever he thought of little Jolie Wheeler.

"You, my friend, are an excellent host."

Carson jerked his attention back to his guest, sitting across from him in the other plump leather armchair in the Raven's Nest library.

Carson lifted his scotch, forcing himself to focus on his goals at hand. "Thank you. I've very much enjoyed having you and your family at Raven's Nest. I hope you feel welcome to use my home anytime, even when I'm not in residence."

"I wonder if you would be as gracious if I decide not to sell you Hertzog Communications."

Carson raised an eyebrow as he refilled the man's drink. "Am I to take that as some sort of announcement?"

Frederick studied him for a long moment while the fire in the grate crackled between them and then he chuckled. "You are a cool one, McRaven. No, it's not an announcement. The truth is, I made my decision before we even came to Raven's Nest. The company is yours if you still want it. Your offer is generous. I know your record and I've seen how you treat other companies you have acquired. I believe you will treat my employees with great care. They are what matters most to me."

He had won. Carson should be celebrating. This was the heady moment he always savored, the taste of victory on his tongue, more potent than even the finest aged scotch.

Right now he felt rather hollow and had an insane wish that he had someone to share the news with.

"Do you not have anything to say?" Frederick asked.

This wasn't turning out the way he expected. He should be jubilant, not fighting this discordant feeling that everything he thought he wanted had been shaken on its head the last few days.

"Sorry. I'm thrilled. Of course I am. Thank you. Your decision is wonderful news, exactly what I had hoped. You can be sure I will do my best to take good care of all you have worked so hard to build over the years. I'll make a call to the attorneys first thing in the morning and have them start the paperwork."

Frederick made an impatient gesture. "It's Christmas. Do you not think that can wait? Let your people enjoy the holiday. My decision won't change between now and December twenty-sixth."

Carson forced a smile, unused to feeling chided, especially by someone he respected as much as he did Frederick Hertzog.

"You're right," he said after a long moment. "All the details can wait until after the holidays."

Frederick studied him while the fire crackled and hummed. "And how are you spending Christmas after we leave in the morning?"

Carson wasn't quite sure how to answer that question. His plans for a long, solitary ride into the mountains on one of the horses would probably seem rather staid and solitary to a man like Frederick Hertzog, who lived for his family.

"I'm not sure yet," he said, which wasn't exactly a lie.

"Ah. Too many choices?"

"Something like that."

Frederick studied him for another long moment, his eyes entirely too perceptive. "Why don't you have a wife? Children?"

Carson shifted in his chair, deeply uncomfortable with this particular line of questioning. "I guess it just hasn't really been a priority in my life."

"And why not? If you don't mind an interfering old-timer's opinion, a man needs family around him, especially as the years flow past. You might think big, beautiful houses and land and more companies are enough for you. But when you get to be the ripe old age of seventy-five, you learn how little those things matter. Family. That's the important thing. The joy of watching your grandchildren grow, of knowing you have raised a good, honorable son, of having your wife by your side and standing by in amazement as she becomes more beautiful in your eyes with every passing day. That is where you find true joy."

Carson gazed into the flickering fire, wishing he could clap his hands over his ears to shut out the other man's words.

What was happening to him this week? He had come to Raven's Nest five days ago, comfortable in the assurance that his life was rolling along exactly on the track he wanted. His company was successful beyond his wildest dreams, he had found the ideal location for his ranch, he had everything he could imagine.

If he sometimes wondered why he was working so hard, he just figured that was part of living the high life.

But somehow everything was changing. All he thought he had attained seemed empty. Meaningless. For the first time, he was beginning to realize how completely he had shut everyone else out of his life. His friendships for the most part were shallow, his relationships with women always casual.

He had become very adept at relying only on himself. Now he was beginning to wonder if he had made a grave mistake.

It wasn't a pleasant realization or a particularly comfortable one.

She was nearly done.

The Hertzogs had left just a short time ago to meet their plane at the Jackson Hole Airport. They planned to fly to Aspen for the final leg of their ski journey and she had sent them on their way with breakfast crostinis, chicken foie gras sausages and rosemary potatoes.

To her surprise, Antonia Hertzog had given her a hug before she left along with a card with her e-mail address, begging Jenna to keep in touch and to send her recipes for several of the dishes she had served.

Frederick Hertzog had shaken her hand. He had solemnly—but with his eyes twinkling—thanked her for preparing meals "as filling to the soul as to the stomach."

Even Amalia had given her a shy smile and whispered her thanks.

Now all Jenna had left was to wash a few more dishes and finish storing the leftovers that could be heated in clearly marked containers for Carson.

She was glad it was over, she told herself. These two days had seemed endless, though she had loved the work. Having the freedom to create meals with unlimited ingredients had been both challenging and immensely rewarding.

She couldn't do it again, though. Even if Carson offered her a private jet of her own to chef for another of his parties, she would have to decline. Two days at Raven's Nest was more than enough. She couldn't work for him again, not with this insane attraction she couldn't seem to quash.

She would find a way, though. Once she was away from him and back in the flow of her regular life, she wouldn't even have time to think about Carson McRaven or the heat of his kiss or the way he made her insides quiver with sensations she thought she had buried with her husband.

Fifteen minutes later, she dried the last serving tray and returned it to the shelf, then gave one last look around the kitchen to make sure she hadn't forgotten anything.

"I suppose you're glad this is over."

She whirled around to find Carson in the doorway. Her heartbeat instantly kicked up a notch, much to her frustration. So much for the assurances she made to herself that she could put her attraction away.

For some reason, she hadn't expected to see him again before she left. They had no business left between them, since his assistant had expressed payment to her the day before. She had already deposited it in the bank and this morning had transferred payment over to her small business loan, much to her delight.

She hadn't really *wanted* to see him. Yet, here he was in jeans and a casual shirt and those disreputable boots again. She sighed and tried to pretend he didn't affect her in the slightest.

"My children are eager to have their mother back so we can get to some of our holiday traditions," she finally answered.

He stepped into the kitchen and leaned a hip against the work island.

"Like what?"

"Oh, the usual. Nothing very exciting, I suppose. Tonight we're going to drive around and look at Christmas lights around town. Tomorrow is Christmas Eve and we're driving to Idaho Falls to pick up my mother-in-law, who'll be staying a few nights with us. We'll probably go to a matinee or something with her and then dinner, then we'll read stories and play games by the fire until the boys are worn out enough to sleep. Which might be quite late this year, I'm afraid. Hayden tells me he plans to stay up until at least eleven o'clock."

She was rambling, she realized. His blue eyes wore an odd expression. Probably glazed over from boredom, she thought, embarrassed.

"That probably sounds excruciatingly dull to you, doesn't it?"

"You might be surprised," he murmured.

She didn't know how to answer that so she changed the subject. "What about you? What are your plans for Christmas?"

"That seems to be the question on everyone's mind. Actually, I have work today and tomorrow."

"On Christmas Eve?"

"I have several projects in the works right now so I thought I would catch up on the research I need to do for them."

How terribly sad, she thought. Instead of celebrating with family and friends, he planned to hole up in this huge, echoing house by himself and read business reports. She couldn't imagine anything more depressing, though perhaps that was exactly the way he wanted to spend his holidays.

"What about Christmas Day?" she asked, though she wasn't quite sure why she was so insistent on finding out his plans.

"I don't know. Not much. I really don't usually celebrate Christmas, to be honest. I would spend the entire time working but it's hard to do that on your own when everyone else is at home doing their holiday thing. I figured I'd take one of the horses up on the ridgeline trail and then come back and have a drink and a long soak in the hot tub."

She studied him for a long moment, struck at the sudden realization that what she had always taken for coldness, for hardness, actually cloaked a great deal of loneliness. Why had she never realized it before?

"You could come to our place for dinner on Christmas, if you'd like." She spoke quickly, regretting the words almost the moment she uttered them.

He straightened from the work island, his eyes astonished. "I didn't realize you were in the habit of inviting strays to dinner."

If he was a stray, he was a sleek, extraordinarily well-groomed one. She colored a little, feeling foolish all over again at the impulsive invitation. She couldn't rescind it now, though, so she plowed forward.

"One more person at the table certainly won't make much of a difference, especially this year. Usually my brother and his family would be there but they're leaving tomorrow morning on a cruise. It will only be my brood and my mother-in-law."

She made a face as she suddenly remembered one salient point that couldn't be overlooked. "I should warn you, in the interest of full disclosure, that Pat—my late husband's mother—can be...difficult. She had a stroke a year ago and she suffered brain damage from it. I'm afraid, well, it's changed her personality a bit. And not for the better, I'm sorry to say. She was always a strong-willed woman but since her stroke, she's become, um…"

Her voice trailed off and she felt disloyal for even bringing it up.

"Mean?" he asked.

She stared. "How did you know that?"

"Hayden told me a few things she's said about me. Not very complimentary things, I'm afraid."

Jenna winced. She could only imagine what Hayden might have told him. Carson and Raven's Nest were two of Pat's favorite targets for vitriol. She couldn't understand Jenna's reasons for selling the ranch to him and Jenna had never been able to explain to her that her comfortable assisted-living center would never have been in their budget if she hadn't.

"I'm sorry. She's actually a wonderful woman most of the time. She just has her moments."

"But you still have her out to your house for Christmas?"

Jenna sighed at his flabbergasted expression. "She has no other family. Joe was her only son and the Wagon Wheel was her home long before it was mine. What else can I do? My children still love her dearly and she never displays cruelty to them."

"Only to you?"

She flashed him a quick look. The man was too blasted perceptive. "Not much. Anyway, if I haven't completely scared you off, you're welcome to join us for dinner. We'll probably eat around four. My boys enjoy your company and even Jolie seems completely smitten. All afternoon yesterday she wouldn't stop saying mister. Which I'm fairly sure meant you since you're the only new man in her life."

He smiled at that and she gazed at the way it seemed to light up his features.

How did he completely wreck all her grand intentions, just with a simple smile? That crazy hunger surged back through her veins and she could only stare at him.

* * *

He had to kiss her again.

The impulse was so overwhelming, he just about gripped the counter's edge to keep from reaching for her.

She was inviting him to share Christmas dinner with her family. With her boys and her darling little girl and her mother-in-law.

Part of him was totally enraptured by the idea. But it terrified him far more.

What did he know about family Christmases? When he was a kid, December twenty-fifth had simply been another day, another excuse for his mother to drink or shoot up until she passed out and he had to clean her up and put her to bed.

He could remember one happy Christmas from his childhood, the year he had spent with his grandparents.

He had become used to treating the day like any other, just a little more inconvenient since the rest of the world seemed to stop. If he spent the day with Jenna and her family, he was very much afraid he would never be able to go back to those quiet, solitary days he told himself he enjoyed.

"Forget it. I should never have invited you." She turned away and he realized he must have been standing there staring at her for a full minute or more.

"It's silly," she went on. "You don't have to feel obligated. Just pretend I never opened my big, stupid mouth."

The big, stupid mouth he couldn't stop thinking about? The one that haunted his dreams, that he could still taste every time he closed his eyes?

"Jenna—"

"Just forget it," she said. "It was a crazy impulse."

"No, it wasn't. It was very sweet."

Her gaze flashed to his, her eyes wide and surprised and he lost the battle for control. He stepped forward, pulled her against him and kissed her, as he had been dreaming about doing since the first time he had tasted her.

She gasped his name just before his mouth found hers. He might have expected her to pull away, as she had done that first time. Instead, she hitched in a little breath and wrapped her arms around his neck and his tenuous hold on control slipped completely away.

She tasted even better than he remembered from the day before, warm and sultry and sweet at the same time, like juicy sugared peaches.

She responded wildly to his kiss and he pressed against her, relishing her curves and the way her breathing came in aroused little gasps. She opened her mouth for his kiss and her tongue tangled with his.

The heat and taste of her sent blood surging to his groin and he was instantly aroused. He gripped her bottom and pulled her against him and she let out a soft, sexy little sound and twisted her fingers in his hair.

They kissed for a long time, until he couldn't think straight and his body ached for more. "Let's go upstairs," he murmured after several drugging moments. "I've got a huge bed in my room. It's far more comfortable than a marble-topped island."

He knew his words were a colossal mistake the moment he said them. She froze in his arms for only an instant but he didn't want to let her go. Not yet. He couldn't let her pull away this time. He lowered his mouth again and after only a moment, she kissed him back with more of that enticing eagerness that took his breath away.

He wanted more. He had to have her, right now, right here, to hell with comfort or common sense.

He slid his hands under her shirt, to the warm skin at her back and trailed his lips from her mouth to her neck then to the creamy, delicious skin at the vee of her shirt.

She gripped his head to hold him in place for a moment, then he was vaguely aware of her hands falling away just as he dipped a tongue beneath her bra, to the lush swell of one breast.

She pushed at him but he couldn't bring himself to heed her, too lost in his hunger.

"Stop, Carson. Oh, please, stop."

Her whispered words finally pierced his subconscious and he froze, frustration whipping through him.

He stepped away from her but couldn't seem to contain the string of low, bitter curses, a throwback to his rough childhood on the street.

She looked shaken to the core, her eyes wide and almost glassy. Not at his language, he realized. At the wild ferocity of their kiss.

He had let things get completely out of his control, something he never did. She had tried to stop, he remembered with considerable self-disgust, but he hadn't wanted to end the kiss until she actually said the words.

He raked a hand through his hair. "Jenna, I'm…"

"Don't say it. Don't you *dare* say you're sorry." Her breath came in sharp little gusts, her chest heaving up and down as she tried to regain control.

He was. He almost couldn't breathe around the regret—as much for kissing her in the first place as for not being willing to stop.

"I was just going to tell you I won't be coming for Christmas dinner. I need to go back to San Francisco."

Now. Today. To hell with the fact that he'd given his pilot the three days off until the holidays were over. He would take a commercial flight if he had to. He needed to return to a place where his life was sane and normal again, instead of filled with adorable toddler urchins, gabby troublemaking boys or lovely widows with big green eyes and kisses that were rapidly becoming his obsession.

"Now who's running away?" she asked quietly. She lifted her hands to repair some of the damage his fingers had done to her careful hairstyle and he saw she was shaking.

He wanted more than anything to touch her again but he

didn't trust himself. "This is insane, Jenna. I'm fiercely attracted to you. More than I've ever been to a woman in my life. I'm not used to…losing control like I just did. I can't let it happen again."

She laughed harshly. "What makes you think I would let you kiss me again?"

He gave her a long look. "Can you do anything to stop it?"

"I just did, didn't I?"

"Eventually. But you didn't want me to stop, did you? Not really."

She just looked at him out of those eyes that suddenly looked bruised and he gave a heavy sigh.

"I don't know what this thing is between us," he said. "But when we kiss, it's like the blowup of a wildfire scorching out of control. It makes absolutely no sense."

"Don't look to me for answers. I don't like it any more than you do."

He needed a clean break from her. That was the only way he could regain any kind of sanity. He needed her and her children out of his life, once and for all—or at least as far out of it as he could manage when they lived just down the hill from Raven's Nest. He didn't like being cruel—the mother-in-law he hadn't even met came to mind—but he couldn't see any other option.

"Look, I'm physically attracted to you, Jenna. I can't deny that. But I never should have kissed you. This was a mistake. I don't want to be attracted to you and I'm sorry I lost control like that. You come with tangles and complications I can't handle. I'm not *interested* in handling them. The whole kid and family thing is not anything I'm looking for and that's what you're all about, isn't it. I'm sorry, but you're just not the kind of woman I want."

She paled a shade or two and he didn't think he had ever despised himself as much as he did right at this moment. "I guess that's clear enough, isn't it?"

"Jenna—"

"No, I appreciate your honesty. I do. And since we're being so up-front and honest with each other, I'll come right out and just say, right back at you. You are absolutely the last man I would be interested in starting anything with. Yes, I find you attractive. But I also believe you're the most manipulative, self-absorbed person I have ever met. You think you have everything you could ever want, but the truth is, your world is cold and empty. I would feel sorry for you except it would be a complete waste of my time and energy, something in short supply in the whole *kid and family thing* I call my life. Goodbye, Mr. McRaven."

She headed for the door and he wanted, more than anything, to apologize, to call her back and tell her he didn't mean any of it. He couldn't, though. Because underneath it all was more than a grain of truth.

He forced himself to say nothing as she grabbed her parka off the hook in the mudroom with a force that nearly ripped it out of the wall, then she stormed out the back door, slamming it hard behind her.

She left an echoing kind of silence between them. The kitchen that had seemed so warm and full of lovely scents when she was there had turned barren, inhospitable.

He stood for a moment, flayed open by her words. *You think you have everything but the truth is, your world is cold and empty. I would feel sorry for you except it would be a complete waste of my time and energy.*

She was exactly right. A week ago, he would have taken great satisfaction in telling her his life was exactly the way he wanted it. Now he didn't know what the hell he wanted.

He needed to get out of there. Now. He pulled out his cell phone to call Carrianne to arrange the details and see how quickly she could find him a way out of the area when he suddenly realized he hadn't seen Jenna's van head down the mountain yet.

He moved to the window overlooking the back driveway and

frowned. What was she doing? Her van was still parked there but Jenna was nowhere in sight. He stood for another moment, baffled at the delay, then with growing uneasiness, he opened the door.

His heart clogged his throat and icy panic crackled through him. She hadn't gone to her van because she hadn't made it beyond the back steps. She was lying crumpled at the bottom of the stairs, her eyes closed and her face deathly white to match the snow drifting down to cover her skin.

Chapter Twelve

He shoved open the door, barely aware of the bitter cold that cut through his clothes or the snowflakes that had turned mean and hard.

He rushed down the steps, then scrambled to grab hold of the handrail when his feet started to slip out from underneath him. Why was it so damn icy? He had installed radiant heat under all the sidewalks and steps leading to the house to melt the snow.

Something must have gone haywire with the system. He suddenly remembered her saying that morning to her sister-in-law and children that the steps were a little icy but he hadn't paid much attention to her words.

In her anger at him, Jenna must have rushed out of the house without remembering her own caution or how treacherous it was.

None of that mattered, he thought as he crouched down beside her still form.

"Jenna?" He reached a hand out to cup her cheek, sick fear curdling in his stomach at the cool fragility of her skin. "Jenna? Come on, sweetheart. Answer me."

She made no response at all. He wanted to shake her awake but he was afraid to move her in case she had a spinal injury. He didn't want to cause any more pain than he had already done.

He took his hand away from her cheek and smoothed her hair away from her pale features. He was almost certain it was his imagination when she moved slightly toward him, as if seeking the warmth of his fingers.

"Come on, Jenna. Wake up and we'll get you home."

She moaned a little but didn't open her eyes. He did a quick physical assessment and saw that one arm was tucked underneath her back. Even with his limited experience, he could see something was drastically wrong with the unnatural position of it.

His fault. All of this was his fault. He had goaded her, had done his best to make her as angry as possible with him for his own self-serving reasons, so he could push her away to the safe distance where he kept everyone else in his life.

He should have known the radiant-heat system wasn't working right but he had been so preoccupied the last few days that he hadn't paid any attention to something as critical as her safety.

Hell, she wouldn't have even *been* at Raven's Nest to fall down his steps if he hadn't forced her to go against her better judgment and bribed her into cooking for his house party.

"I'm sorry, Jenna. Just wake up and I'll make it better. Come on." He squeezed her fingers, trying desperately not to remember the last time he had begged a woman he cared about to wake up, eighteen years ago as he watched Suzanna slip into a coma as a result of her eclampsia.

"Damn it, Jenna. Wake up," he ordered, his voice harsher than he intended. "Your kids are waiting for you at home. They need you right now."

That did the trick. She moaned a little more but blinked her eyes open.

Relief coursed through him, hot and fierce. On a purely rational level, he was quite certain it hadn't been more than a minute or so since he opened the back door and found her lying on the steps, but he felt as if he had lived through two or three lifetimes in that miserable span of time.

She moaned a little more and tried to rise to a seated position but he gently pressed a hand to her chest to hold her in place.

"Don't try to move yet, at least until we can figure out what kind of damage you've done."

She blinked up at him like a sleepy kitten. "What…what happened?"

"I didn't see, but I can guess. You must have slipped on the icy steps. Apparently the radiant-heating system isn't working the way it's supposed to. Looks like you must have taken quite a header."

She touched her right hand to the back of her head then moved as if to lift the other arm from beneath her and he saw raw pain spasm across her features.

"Ow! Ow, ow, ow."

Her distressed cry just about broke his heart. "I know. You've hurt your wrist pretty badly. We're going to get some help. What else hurts? I tried to do a quick assessment but I don't really know what I'm looking for."

Her lovely features contorted with pain. "Head. Arm. Ankle."

"I'd say that about covers it. Okay. I left my phone inside. I'm just going to grab it and a blanket for you while I call the ambulance. I'll be back before you know it, okay? Just hold still."

Despite his order, she pushed up with her good arm until she was sitting on the icy step, her hand pressed to the back of her head and the other arm hanging loosely at an awkward angle. "I'm okay. Don't call an ambulance."

"You are very far from okay, Jenna. You've taken a terrible fall."

"Freezing."

He didn't think she had any spinal injuries and he hated the idea of her having to sit out here in the snow while he called for help. Since she had already taken it upon herself to sit up, he supposed there was no harm in taking her in the house.

"Come on. Let's get you where it's warm."

He carefully scooped her into his arms, wondering how she could feel so delicate and be so stubborn at the same time. Her back was cold where she had been lying on the icy steps and he felt sick inside all over again.

He carried her to the sitting area of the kitchen and pulled a knit throw off the corner of the sofa, then turned the gas fireplace on high.

"Don't call an ambulance," she repeated when he crossed the kitchen for his phone. He was relieved to hear she was already sounding more like herself. "I twisted my ankle and bunged up my arm. You don't need to bother the volunteer paramedics with a silly thing like that. They have much more important things to worry about."

Nothing is more important than making sure you're okay, he wanted to say, but he knew he would sound ridiculous.

He could see the determination in her eyes and knew she would not appreciate it if he went against her wishes and called the ambulance anyway.

"Okay," he finally said. "We'll do things your way. I can take you to the hospital in Jackson Hole or the one in Idaho Falls. Your choice."

"Neither. I don't need to go to the hospital."

"Pick one." He could be just as stubborn as Jenna Wheeler and it was high time she realized that.

"Fine," she grumbled. "Jake Dalton at the clinic in town can take care of this. I would appreciate it if you could drive me there."

She looked as if the words just about choked her. Under less stressful circumstances, he might have smiled, but he had a feeling it would be a long time before he found anything amusing, especially since all he could think about was that terrible moment when he had opened the kitchen door and found her lying so still on his steps.

"If you know the number, I'll call and let them know we're on our way."

She gave it to him and he punched it into his phone, thinking he would just call after they were on the road. "Be sure to tell Jake I have to stop at my house first and make sure the kids are still okay."

"We'll call them on the way."

"Carson—"

"Brace yourself." He scooped her up again.

"Honestly," she exclaimed. "This is *not* necessary."

"Says you."

"I can walk if you put me down." Her voice was muffled and he was glad to see color returning to her features. He held her tighter, knowing he shouldn't be enjoying this so much. It seemed slightly warped when she was in such pain that he could find such contentment just having her in his arms.

"It's this or the ambulance. Which would you prefer?"

"Neither," she muttered.

"Too bad," he said as he reached the garage. "I'm not taking any chances, Jenna. You took a hard fall and that wrist looks seriously injured and I can already tell your ankle is going to swell."

"I don't have time for this," she wailed. "Tomorrow is Christmas Eve!"

Guilt pinched at him as he set her in the backseat of the ranch's Suburban. She had wanted to make the holiday idyllic for her children. He remembered her telling him about the last rough two Christmases and how things had to be just right this year.

How was she ever going to do that, battered and sore as she was now?

And how was he ever going to forgive himself for ruining the perfect holiday she had planned out so carefully?

An hour later, Jake Dalton pursed his mouth as he looked at computerized X-rays. "Well, Jen, you've done a real job on yourself."

"I know. I'm such a klutz."

He grinned. "How would I ever pay my bills if not for klutzes like you? I'd be out of a job."

She made a face at him. She knew perfectly well Jake Dalton was probably the most underpaid doctor in Idaho. He opened his clinic at least two days a month for people who didn't have health insurance and he and his wife, Maggie, spent several weeks every summer volunteering in poverty-stricken areas in Central America.

As much as she liked and admired Jake and considered Maggie one of her closest friends, she would rather be just about anywhere else on earth right now than sitting in one of his exam rooms in a hospital gown.

"So do you want the good news or the bad news first?" Jake asked.

"I hate when you say that. Give me the good news first, I guess, so I have something positive to think about while you give me the bad news."

"Well, you've got a mild concussion."

"That's the good news?"

"It could be worse, darlin'. And I'm happy to report that your ankle's not broken, only sprained. You're going to have to stay off it for a day or two but you should be dancing by New Year's Eve."

"I suppose that's something. What about my wrist? Is that the bad news?"

"You could say that. Take a look." He swiveled the computer monitor around so she could see the screen. If the drugs his nurse practitioner wife gave her hadn't already been making her woozy, the X-ray would have done the job. She could clearly see the jagged bones sticking out at an odd angle.

"I guess I'll be in a cast for Christmas. It could be worse, right?"

Jake's face grew solemn. "Jenna, I'm about ninety-nine percent sure you're going to need surgery. That's the bad news I was talking about. This looks beyond something I can take care of here in the office, just because of the break's location. I'm going to get on the phone with the hospital in Idaho Falls and see if they can schedule you in today or tomorrow."

She thought of all her plans, of looking at Christmas lights and reading stories and Christmas dinner with her children's remaining grandparent. "No. No way. Jake, tomorrow's Christmas Eve. I can't ruin this for my kids again."

"I'm afraid you don't have much choice in the matter, at least about the surgery. But nobody said it has to ruin anybody's Christmas. It's most likely an outpatient surgery. You could have it done first thing in the morning and be home by early afternoon."

"Couldn't you just cast it and let me have the surgery after Christmas? Please, Jake." She pleaded with him as a neighbor and as a friend. "I swore to myself I wouldn't let anything ruin Christmas for my boys and for Jolie. You know what it's been like for us. Two years ago Joe was dying and then last year we were dealing with Pat's stroke and Jolie's pneumonia. I can't do the hospital thing again. Everything has to be perfect this year."

"Nothing's perfect, Jenna."

"I know that. I just don't want to see the inside of a hospital this Christmas."

He studied her for a long moment and then he sighed. "You're a hard woman to say no to. Has Maggie been giving you lessons?"

She smiled. "It's a gift we share. What can I say?"

"Look, I can try to set it here. I'm not sure we can put the bones back into the right position but we can try. It won't be easy."

What in her life was? Jenna thought. "Thanks, Jake. I just need to make it through Christmas and then you can do all the surgeries you want."

"I don't want to do *any* surgeries. My preference would be to have you home safe and sound without mild concussions or sprained ankles or anything."

She nodded, grateful beyond words that Jake had decided to come back to Pine Gulch to practice medicine. He could have taken a job anywhere but he had opted to become a family physician in his own hometown and the entire town owed him a huge debt for it.

"This is going to take a while and we'll have to get you good and loopy. Are your kids okay?"

She hoped so. She had called them on the way here and all seemed to be under control, but with her children, that could change in an instant. "Yes. Erin's with them and Terri said she would run out and help her."

"What about a ride home? Can McRaven stick around and wait for you? You'll be in no shape to drive for a while."

"You can send him home," she said. "Terri or my brother can give me a ride back up the canyon."

"I'll do my best. But I've got to tell you, the man looks pretty settled out there in the waiting room. I don't think he's going anywhere. Let's get you into the procedure room then I'll go talk to McRaven."

Sure enough, Jake returned a few moments later with Maggie and an ominous tray of medical implements—and the news that Carson insisted on staying until her arm was set and casted.

Jenna wanted to protest, but the medication Maggie had given her for the pain was making her far too muddleheaded to think straight.

The next hour passed in a blur. Jake first made sure her entire arm was numb and she was blissfully chatting with Maggie about shoes and shopping and the Daltons' two-year-old, Ada, who was currently spending the afternoon with her grandmother.

Afterward, she vaguely recalled Jake warning her to keep her head averted while he worked the pieces of bone together, then enduring another X-ray to make sure everything was set correctly.

She also had random snatches of memory of Maggie helping

Jake cast her arm in a festive red, which she assured them she had to have so she could match her new Christmas dress.

Finally, Jake told her he would drop by her house to check on her the next morning and she was to come back the day after Christmas for another X-ray so they could see if the bones were staying the way he set them.

In the meantime, she was also under strict instructions to stay off her sprained ankle.

"I would give you crutches," Jake said, "but having one arm in a cast makes getting around on them a little difficult. You'll have to use a cane and just be on your honor that you'll keep the weight off that foot."

Jenna nodded, wondering how in the heck she was going to cook Christmas dinner when she couldn't stand up. She would figure something out, she thought. She always did.

Carson jumped up the moment Jake wheeled her into the waiting room and she flushed, embarrassed that he had hung around for her longer than an hour in a room full of crying babies and sniffly children.

"What are you still doing here? My brother or his wife could have given me a ride. Now I've ruined your whole day."

"The day's not over yet," Carson said with a smile and Jenna could swear she heard several of the young mothers in the waiting room give dreamy sighs.

"So you're good to go?" he asked.

She looked to Jake for confirmation. "Just make sure you take the pain pills I gave you on schedule," the physician said sternly. "Don't try to be a hero or I promise, you'll suffer for it later."

She nodded, suddenly weak with exhaustion as Carson took over behind the wheelchair and pushed her out the door toward his black SUV.

She must have dozed off on the six-mile drive up the canyon. She didn't awaken until he pulled up in front of her house and turned off the engine, when the cessation of noise and movement jerked her out of sleep.

The smell of leather and enticing male filled her senses and she blinked her eyes open, to realize that somehow in her sleep she had moved across the seat and was resting her head on his shoulder.

Out of sheer instinct, she jerked her head away, then gasped when pain cut through her like a buzz saw. The acute nature of her wrist and ankle injuries had taken center stage the last hour. Somehow she had forgotten the crack her head had taken and the concussion that had resulted from it.

Still, she made herself pull away from Carson. "Sorry. I didn't mean to fall asleep on you." And she meant that quite literally.

He smiled that devastating smile again. "Don't worry about it. I'm glad my shoulder was here. I thought about just driving so you could rest but I figured you would feel better when you were home."

"I do need to get back to my children. I've been away too long as it is."

He studied her for a long moment and she saw something that looked suspiciously like guilt flicker across his features. "You know you're going to need help, right?" he finally said. "Is there anyone you can call?"

Panic flickered through her whenever she thought about how much her injury complicated her already hectic life, but she ruthlessly shoved it down. "Hayden and Drew can help me."

He raised an eyebrow. "They're just kids. They're not going to know what to do if you start speaking in tongues in the middle of the night from that bump on your head."

"We'll be fine, Carson," she assured him with far more confidence than she felt. "Thank you for giving me a ride to the clinic and for everything."

She suddenly remembered quite clearly the conversation they had been having just before she foolishly stomped out of his house and ended up slipping down the stairs.

You come with tangles and complications I can't handle. I'm not interested in handling them. The whole kid and family thing is not anything I'm looking for and that's what you're all about, isn't it. I'm sorry, but you're just not the kind of woman I want.

How humiliating. She makes a grand, door-slamming exit, intending never to see the man again, and then ends up falling flat on her butt. Now here he was, hours later, forced to babysit her.

Could their relationship become any more awkwardly entangled?

"I really do appreciate the ride," she repeated.

She started to open the car door but he shoved out of his seat and hurried around the vehicle before she could even get it open.

When he jerked the door open, his eyes glittered with annoyance and his mouth was hard and tight.

"You're crazy. That's the only explanation that makes sense. I thought you were just stubborn but I've finally figured out that you're just plain nuts."

She shrugged. She should probably be offended, but she just didn't have the energy right now. "I'm a mother. It's part of the job description."

"Well, crazy or not, I'm not letting you hobble into the house by yourself and I'm not letting you stay here alone. You obviously can't be trusted to take care of yourself, so somebody needs to keep an eye on you, somebody bigger than four feet tall."

"Who did you have in mind?"

His smile was as dangerous as a crouched mountain lion. "I can bunk on your couch."

She stared at him, "Now who's the crazy one? You can't stay here."

"Watch me."

"Carson, tomorrow is Christmas Eve. The last place on earth you want to be is in my crowded house with four jacked-up kids."

Something odd flickered in the depths of his eyes, something she couldn't quite read.

"We'll all have to adapt, won't we? I won't back down on this, Jen. You were hurt at my house, on my watch, and that makes me responsible for you."

"You can set your mind at ease. I fell down the stairs. It was completely an accident. I'm not the sort who will sue you or anything, especially for something that was my own blasted fault."

"I don't care about the legalities."

"I'm sure your McRaven lawyers would love to hear you say that."

"Screw the lawyers. This is deeper than that. I'm responsible for what happened to you. I intend to make sure you're in capable hands."

She shivered a little, remembering just how capable those hands had been earlier. When she caught the direction of her thoughts, she flushed and blamed her reaction on either the lingering exhaustion or the painkillers Jake had given her.

She was too tired to argue with him right now, she decided. She would figure it all out after she had rested and could think straight again.

"Fine. You have no idea what you're walking into but I'm too woozy-headed to talk any sense into you right now. But just remember when you've got kids hanging off you and your head is splitting that I warned you what to expect."

Chapter Thirteen

She did warn him.

Two hours later, Carson stood in Jenna's compact kitchen trying to scrub burned macaroni and cheese off her stove top. Behind him at the kitchen table, Jolie in her high chair was starting to fret and rub her eyes and Kip was gabbing a mile a minute about all the things he wanted Santa to bring him the next night, though for the life of him, Carson couldn't figure out who the kid was talking to.

His brothers certainly weren't paying him any attention. Hayden and Drew were arguing about everything under the sun, from the best place to go fishing in the summer to how to throw a spitball to which of them was better at *Super Mario Galaxy*.

He was quite certain his head was going to explode in another sixty seconds.

What the hell was he thinking, imagining even for a moment that he could handle this?

The Wii argument was quickly getting out of hand and he finally had to step in. "Guys. Guys. Come on. Your mom's going to wake up if you keep at each other's throats like this."

Drew instantly backed down. "Sorry, Mr. McRaven," he said.

As he might have expected, Hayden wasn't nearly so cooperative. "Why do we have to listen to you?" he asked in that surly tone Carson had become used to, though he took some small degree of satisfaction that the boy had forgotten to cop his attitude for a large part of the afternoon. Apparently the temporary cease-fire was over.

"You shouldn't even be here," Hayden groused.

Damn straight, he shouldn't. He couldn't have agreed more with the boy. He was completely out of his element here. But he had given Jenna his word and right now he didn't see any other alternative.

At least she wasn't around to see how miserably he was failing her. Jenna had fallen asleep a few hours ago—and he was amazed she had made it as long as she had. When he carried her inside the house, she had insisted he set her on the living room couch in front of their lopsided Christmas tree.

Anyone looking in on the scene might have guessed she had been away from her children for weeks, the way none of them wanted to let her out of their sights. At first he thought they were extraordinarily clingy, until he remembered how frightening the situation must have seemed from their standpoint, children who lost their father just two Christmases ago.

She hadn't seemed to mind having them right there with her. While Carson stood by feeling helpless, she had talked with them for a good half hour even while he could see her energy begin to wane.

Before he could usher the children out of the living room, she was fast asleep, as she had been for the last two hours.

"Look, your mom needs rest," he reminded her boys and the darling little cherub in the high chair with the orange cheese sauce mustache. "I know she'll want to be feeling better tomorrow for Christmas Eve so we all need to give her the chance to take it easy while she can."

"We were supposed to go look at Christmas lights tonight,"

Kip said with a pout. "My friend Cody says his house has more lights than anyone in Pine Gulch and I want to go see it."

He thought about piling them all into his Suburban and driving into town. It would be a distraction, anyway, and might put Jolie to sleep. On the other hand, the logistics of loading them all in overwhelmed him—quite a humiliating realization for a man who owned dozens of companies and managed to keep track of each one of them.

"Are you still going to be here on Christmas Eve?" Hayden asked crossly.

"I don't know," he answered. *Lord, I hope not.* "I guess that will depend on your mom and how she's doing."

The words were barely out of his mouth when the woman in question appeared in the doorway looking pale and rumpled. Her hair was a little disheveled but she still looked as lovely as ever.

He didn't know when he had ever seen a more welcomed sight. Apparently her children shared his sentiment.

"Mommy!" Kip exclaimed and rushed to his mother.

Carson didn't miss her wince as the boy collided with her but she quickly hid it and enveloped him in her arms. A weird ache quivered in his chest as he watched the two of them. She had to be feeling like she'd been run over by a truck right about now, but she still let her little kid maul her.

"I'm sorry." She pushed a stray lock of hair out of her eyes. "I didn't mean to sleep so long. I didn't mean to sleep at all, actually."

"With all the meds they filled you with at the doc's, it's a wonder you lasted as long as you did."

She made a face. "I hate the stuff. I wish I could have convinced Jake that a couple of aspirin would do just fine for me."

"Mommy hurt," Jolie said. She looked adorably empathetic, her little chin quivering as if she was going to cry, too.

Jenna hobbled to her high chair and leaned down to press a soft kiss on the top of her daughter's curls. "Just a little, baby."

"We had macaroni and cheese," Kip announced. "Only it

wasn't the good kind like you make with the gooey cheese and the crumbly top."

"Sorry," Carson muttered. "I did my best, but apparently I don't have your skills in the kitchen."

He was the CEO of one of the leading tech innovation companies in the world. He shouldn't feel like a complete loser just because he could only make mac and cheese out of a box.

He would have felt about three inches tall if he hadn't caught Jenna's eyes and seen a glowing light there when she looked at him.

"You did great, Carson. Actually, I'm amazed you're still here and haven't run screaming from the house."

"I was tempted a few times."

Her smile was warm and grateful and he told himself the ache in his gut was just hunger. "I can't thank you enough for sticking around. I'm only sorry I fell asleep and left you on your own. That wasn't in the plan."

"You needed it, just like you need to get off that bad foot. Come and sit down and I can get you a bowl of this orange gunk."

"Mmmm. Sounds delicious." She smiled again at him and he was astounded that she could still smile when he knew her pain pills had to be wearing off.

She slid onto the empty chair at the table and he dished up a bowl of the macaroni and cheese and set it in front of her. He found it to be a strange turn of events after the last few days that now he was the one feeding her.

"Thanks. I'm suddenly starving. Even for orange gunk."

His stomach rumbled and he realized he hadn't eaten anything since the breakfast she had served him and the Hertzogs that morning. He dished some onto a plate for himself and slid onto a seat of his own at the table across from her.

It had been years since he'd had the boxed stuff, but to his surprise, it wasn't that bad, especially if a man was hungry enough.

He was further surprised that the boys actually stopped

fighting and sat in relative peace around the table with them while they ate.

"What did you do while I was sleeping?" Jenna asked.

"We went downstairs and played foosball and video games," Drew said. "It was super fun."

"Only because you whipped me six ways to Sunday at *Wii Sports*."

Drew giggled and the sound tugged a reluctant smile out Carson. He had to admit, he had enjoyed that part of the afternoon.

He had been filled with panic when Jenna fell asleep but he discovered the boys were actually quite funny and didn't require much more than a peacekeeper. He found it remarkable that each was such a distinct personality.

And Jolie was a major snuggler. She hadn't wanted to leave his lap, which made swinging a Wii tennis racket a little tough.

"You played all afternoon and then you came up and fixed dinner and everything. I'm really embarrassed I slept so long."

"Don't be. You needed it."

"We tried to be quiet so we didn't wake you up," Drew assured her.

"Some of us did, anyway," Hayden muttered with a dark look to Kip, who Carson had discovered never met a quiet moment he didn't try to fill with chatter.

"I tried," his brother exclaimed. "It's just hard for me."

Carson's gaze met Jenna's and he smiled. As he watched, color crept up her high cheekbones. Why? he wondered, even as that hunger he had been fighting surged up inside him again.

She looked slight and fragile and he still had a hard time believing she was the mother to the four children around the table.

"And we did our chores, Mom, without you even having to nag us," Drew added. "We fed the ponies and Frannie and then we shoveled the snow while Mr. McRaven fixed dinner for us."

"I'm impressed," she told Carson. "What sort of magic obedience school did you send them to while I was sleeping?"

He laughed. "That's my secret." He decided not to tell her he had promised them if they did what he asked, he would get them a copy of a cutting-edge video game one of his companies was creating. It might be bribery, but, hey, a man had to use the tools at his disposal.

Before she could press him, Jolie yawned suddenly, a wide, ear-popping stretch of her jaw, and Jenna instantly went into Mommy mode.

"You're exhausted, aren't you, munchkin?" She pushed away the rest of her mac and cheese. "Let's get you to bed. All of you."

The boys grumbled and looked as if they wanted to argue but Carson shook his head with a pointed look to cut them off before they could even start.

"What do I need to do?" he asked Jenna.

She looked confused and a bit befuddled at how quickly her boys fell into line. "The boys can all shower on their own but Jolie needs a bath. Do you think you can help me with that?"

The thought terrified the hell out of him but he had promised to help her. He couldn't just pick and choose the jobs in his personal comfort zone.

"Sure. You'll have to walk me through it, I'm afraid. Bathing little kids isn't exactly in my skill set."

She smiled. "You're in luck, then, because it is in mine. Boys, take turns in the shower and then meet back here in half an hour for our story."

How was it humanly possible for a man to look so utterly, adorably masculine while he tried to figure out how to put a diaper on a little girl?

Jenna sat on the chair Carson had brought in from the kitchen for her and tried to oversee as best she could. It proved tougher than she had anticipated. He really meant it when he said he didn't know what he was doing.

Sitting on the sidelines was frustrating—but a bit amusing, she had to admit.

"No, the tabs go on the back. You slide that section underneath her bottom and then bring those sides around to connect at the front. Yes, that's the way. You did it!"

He looked ridiculously pleased with himself, even as lopsided as the diaper was. She feared Jolie's entire bedding would be soaked before morning. But she had learned early in her marriage that the quickest way to ensure her husband never helped around the house was to criticize the way he did things— or more subversive and destructive, to go behind him and redo things to her satisfaction.

He struggled to put the pink footie pajamas on until she explained her trick of putting the foot without the zipper on first, then the other foot and the arms last. When he zipped her up, Jolie clapped her hands and beamed at him with her wide, toothy grin. Poor Carson looked so bemused, Jenna could tell her daughter had already bewitched him.

She considered it a minor miracle that the boys bathed and put on their pajamas without turning the house into a major battlefield. They did bicker about whose turn it was to open the wrapped storybook for the night.

Tonight's turned out to be one of their favorites, *How the Grinch Stole Christmas,* much to the boys' glee.

"Are you sure you're up to this? Do you want me to read the story?" Carson asked.

"Not a chance. It's my favorite part of the day."

Jenna took a seat on the sofa by the fireplace in the living room with Jolie in her lap while the boys gathered around. Carson took the easy chair by the Christmas tree, much to her surprise.

Jolie fell asleep round about the time the Grinch was dressing Max the dog in his reindeer antlers. Her soft, warm weight was sweet comfort against her. Even though she ached just about everywhere, she wanted the peace of the moment to go on forever.

She glanced over at Carson and found him watching her out of those fathomless blue eyes.

It seemed oddly right to have him there.

Ridiculous, she told herself. He didn't belong here. He was Carson McRaven of McRaven Enterprises. He had a private jet while she had a Dodge minivan with bald tires. He was only doing her a favor by helping her out while she was injured and she would do well not to put any more importance to it than that.

She finished the last page and closed the book.

"We're almost done with the books!" Kip exclaimed. "That means Santa Claus comes tomorrow night!"

Jenna gave an inward wince as she thought of all the presents she still needed to wrap and the stockings that needed to be filled. She nodded. "I know. We have a lot to do tomorrow to get the house ready for him and I'm going to need everybody's help."

"Is *he* still going to be here in the morning?" Hayden asked, with a head jerk toward Carson.

"By *he,* do you mean Mr. McRaven, who has been kind enough to feed you dinner and play foosball and Wii with you?"

"Yeah. Him."

She glanced at Carson but he appeared unoffended by her son's rudeness. "I don't know. We'll have to see what happens tomorrow. Now into bed, guys. Say your prayers and turn off your lights."

They grumbled a bit but after Carson cleared his throat, they quickly subsided. She wondered how on earth was he doing that and could he teach her? as the boys trudged up the stairs to their rooms.

Carson rose. "Let me carry her upstairs for you."

She knew she couldn't argue. "Thanks. I'm not sure I could do it one-handed."

"Not with your cane, anyway."

He scooped Jolie out of her arms a bit awkwardly and she was aware of the heat of his hands as he brushed her chest in the process. "Which one is her bedroom?"

"The pink one. First door on the left."

He nodded and headed for the stairs and she was astonished at the tenderness that welled up inside her as she saw Carson—big and rangy—holding her small, fatherless child with such gentleness.

She didn't think she could hop up the stairs so she opted to scoot after him on her bottom. He stepped out of Jolie's room just as she reached the top of the stairs, wishing for a little dignity.

He frowned at her. "What do you think you're doing?"

"I need to tuck in my boys," she said.

He rolled his eyes but held a hand out to help her to her feet—or foot, anyway. She hobbled into the room Kip and Drew shared and kissed them each in turn then went across the hall to Hayden's football-maniac room, with its huge Broncos posters on the walls and the orange, blue and white theme that was everywhere she looked.

He looked a little disgruntled that Carson was there as well but she was pleased that he still let her kiss him and tuck the blankets around his shoulders. Her oldest was going to be a teenager before she knew it. How much longer would he let his mother kiss him and rub his hair? Forever, she hoped.

"Night, bud. Thanks for your help today. I don't know what I would do without you," she whispered as she kissed him. His cheeks turned a little rosy and she could tell he was pleased.

"I'm not letting you scoot down the stairs again," Carson said after they closed the door to Hayden's room.

She caught her breath as he scooped her into his arms with effortless ease. He carried her down the stairs without even breathing hard.

She was breathing hard enough for both of them, though she did her best to hide her reaction. She didn't want to admit how truly wonderful it felt to be held like this, to be cherished and watched over.

It was only natural. She had been alone for two years, had been forced to rely only on herself for everything her family needed, from mowing the lawn to taking the car to be fixed to repairing a leaky faucet. The chance to lean on someone else for a change shouldn't seduce her so completely, but she felt powerless to control it.

Downstairs, he set her back on the couch and she forced herself to recall his words that morning, a moment that now seemed a lifetime ago.

She wasn't the kind of woman he wanted. He had told her so, straight-out and she couldn't forget it.

"Where's the best place for me to bunk tonight?"

"This is silly, Carson. You don't need to stay here. Hayden and Drew and I should be able to handle things. I don't need a keeper."

His sigh stirred the air between them. "Do we really have to argue about this again? You've got a concussion, a broken wrist and a sprained ankle. How could I possibly feel comfortable leaving you here alone to deal with four kids by yourself, especially with those heavy-duty painkillers on board? Now where's the best place for me to bunk?"

She wanted to argue, but she could clearly see by the stubborn set of his features that he wasn't going anywhere. And as tough as it was to admit, she felt more comfortable having another adult in the house. The painkillers left her loopy and she couldn't go up and down the stairs if, God forbid, the house caught fire or something. Her pride recoiled at needing his help but since the situation was beyond her control right now, she would just have to accept it with as much grace as possible.

"There's a guest room just off the kitchen. It's the room my mother-in-law uses when she visits."

Just another stress she would have to figure out in the morning, she thought with an edge of panic.

"That should be perfect," Carson said.

They lapsed into silence broken only by the crackle of the fire. Outside she could see snowflakes drifting down. It would have been an idyllic scene if not for the undercurrents that ebbed and flowed between them. She couldn't seem to stop thinking about their kiss in his kitchen that morning or the devastating scene that followed it.

"All right," he finally said. "Out with it. I can see your mind is whirling."

She flushed. "Oh, you're psychic now?"

He shrugged. "You have to be a little omniscient when you buy and sell tech companies. But I don't have to be psychic to see those wheels turning. Your face is remarkably expressive, in case you didn't know."

What else could he read on her face? she wondered. Could he see the slow heat she couldn't seem to control around him?

"Joe used to accuse me of having the worst poker face in eastern Idaho."

"You might as well play your hand, Jenna. What's on your mind?"

Of course, she couldn't tell him what she had been thinking so she quickly made something up. "I, um, was just wondering how long before the boys will safely be asleep. Hayden and Kip usually go right to sleep the minute their lights go out, but Drew has a tendency to read under his covers until I catch him at it and make him turn off the flashlight."

"He pick that up from you or his dad?"

She made a face "Me. I used to do the exact same thing. There are still nights I stay up entirely too late caught up in a good book."

She paused and something about the quiet intimacy of the night made her admit, "It helps to keep the darkness away."

His features softened with sympathy and she instantly regretted her openness. She quickly changed the subject. "Anyway, I still have a few last-minute gifts from Santa to wrap. I need to make sure the boys are all asleep beyond a doubt before I dig them out."

He arched one of those expressive eyebrows. "And how do you expect to wrap presents? With your teeth?"

Her arm ached as if on cue and she gazed down at her cast with no small amount of consternation. "Oh, dear. I hadn't thought that far ahead."

"I can help. I can't guarantee the kind of job I'll do since wrapping presents is another one of those things out of my skill set but I can do my best."

"I can't ask you to do that. You've done enough, Carson. I'll figure something out. Maybe Santa just won't wrap everything this year."

He made an impatient gesture. "Where are your presents and the wrapping paper?"

There was no dissuading the man when he had his mind made up about something and Jenna decided to admit defeat. "We need to make completely sure nobody will be sneaking down the stairs first. Let's give them a few moments and then I'll direct you to my secret stash."

Chapter Fourteen

Carson knew damn well he shouldn't be enjoying this so much.

This wasn't at all how he intended to spend the holidays. He had come to his ranch for two reasons—to host the Hertzogs and to enjoy a little solitude before he returned to the hectic pace of San Francisco.

He certainly never planned to find himself in Jenna Wheeler's comfortable TV room watching *It's a Wonderful Life* on a twenty-inch screen he could barely see and wrapping up action figures.

There were certainly worse ways to pass the time, he had to admit.

"I hope I'm doing this right. I'm not a great gift wrapper."

"They look great." She smiled at him from the couch. "Anyway, the kids don't really care how fancy they look. I doubt they'll even notice. They'll rip all your hard work to pieces in about ten seconds flat."

A weird pang of longing pinched at him. He would like to see Christmas morning at the Wheeler house. The joy and excitement on their faces, the noise and confusion. It would be a completely foreign experience for him but one he suddenly wanted to endure, as crazy as that seemed.

"You know, I can change this," Jenna said, interrupting his thoughts. "You've probably seen this movie a million times."

"Actually, no. I've only seen bits and pieces of it and that was several years ago."

She exaggerated an expression of horror that made him smile. "How can that be? It's completely unnatural."

His smile faded. He thought about making a joke but decided to tell her the truth. "I didn't exactly have the Bedford Falls kind of upbringing."

She gave him a careful look, as if she knew exactly how tough that was for him to admit. "No?"

She was clearly waiting for more. Now that he had opened the door, he wasn't sure he wanted all that information about himself to come slithering out. But the soft compassion in her eyes tugged the words from him.

"My dad ran off before I was born and my mother struggled with depression and drug addiction most of my life. I guess you could say my childhood was on the chaotic side. Foster homes. Shelters. Back and forth with my mom when she would clean up for a while. I spent some time on my grandparents' ranch not far from here, near Ashton. Bill and Nedda Jameson."

Her brow wrinkled with concentration. "Those names seem so familiar. Wait, I think I knew your grandparents. They used to come into my dad's feed store when I was a kid. I remember your grandfather always had Brach's toffee in his pocket."

He smiled a little at the memory. He had adored his grandparents and would have been happy living at their little ranch forever. But his mother hadn't been on good terms with her parents for years and she became furious when she found out they had applied for permanent custody of him. She came to his school one blustery March afternoon and took him away from Idaho and he had never seen Bill or Nedda again.

He had sneaked a few phone calls to them that first year but Lori always found out and made him sorry enough that he had given up and lost touch with them over the years. The first time he had tried to run away at thirteen, he had called and received a recorded message that the number had been disconnected. He later learned they had died the year before within six months of each other—and that they had never stopped trying to find him.

He pushed the grim memories away. "What about you? I bet you watch this every year, right?"

She shook her head. "Joe never liked it. He said it was so sappy it made his teeth stick together." She smiled a little. "He wasn't as crazy about Christmas as I've always been, though he was a good sport when I went wild decorating the house and baking up a storm for weeks beforehand."

He was astonished suddenly at the jealousy that suddenly pierced him at the thought of the happy years she shared with her husband.

"You must miss him a lot."

She flashed him a quick look and then focused her gaze on the screen. He thought she wasn't going to answer but after a moment she muted the television. "He was a good man and a wonderful father. For the first year, I didn't know how I would go on by myself. But I've learned that everything gets a little easier the more time goes on."

He remembered those first few months after Suzanna and Henry James died, when he was certain every particle of light had been sucked out of his world. Gradually the light found holes to peek through, first tiny pinpricks, then bigger and bigger and he learned that life moved on.

She smiled. "It's Christmas. I certainly don't want to forget Joe—I could never do that—but mostly I want to focus this year on all my many blessings. I have four beautiful children, a roof over our heads that's paid for, good neighbors and friends and a supportive family. I've got a business that's taking off the ground. I'm so richly blessed."

She embraced life, Carson realized. Many women would have used what she had endured as an excuse to be embittered, hardened. But Jenna was like a bright beacon of light to those around her. He had seen it at his house party. The Hertzogs had all responded to her because she glowed with life.

Many in the world would consider him the more richly blessed of the two of them, at least materially. He had enjoyed enormous business success, owned houses in three states, had loyal employees. That was only the start. When was the last time he had taken the time to catalogue all he had or even to spend a moment appreciating it?

He felt small and petty and ungrateful.

He turned back to the gifts, wrapping a pile of books he assumed were for Drew. They lapsed into a not uncomfortable silence, their attention on the movie.

"All done," Carson said sometime later when he finished wrapping the last present in the box, a pretty pink-and-white doll for Jolie. Jenna didn't respond and he looked over and saw her eyes were closed and her breathing even.

She had been through a hell of a day. No wonder she fell asleep just minutes before Clarence the angel earned his wings.

He watched her sleep for a long moment, struck by her fragile loveliness and astounded all over again that it covered such indomitable strength.

She needed to eat more of her own cooking. A few of those divine desserts she made would certainly put a little more meat on those thin bones.

A strange feeling stirred up inside him as he watched her sleep. Something tender and gentle and terrifying. He drew in a sharp breath and did his best to shove it back down in the deep, dark recesses of his heart.

"Jenna? Let's get you up to your bed."

She blinked awake slowly and when her gaze met his, she gifted him with a soft smile so free and unfeigned it took his breath away. To his vast regret, it faded as she returned to full consciousness.

"Sorry to wake you but I figured you would be more comfortable where you can stretch out in your own bed," he said.

"I would. Thanks." She sat and moved as if to stand up but he held out a hand to stop her.

"Don't even think about it. You're going to be in serious trouble if you put your weight on that foot."

She gave him a challenging look. "Will I?"

"Yes. The doc told you stay off it, remember? I'll carry you up again," he said, though he almost didn't trust himself to touch her with these emotions churning through him.

"I can scoot up the stairs."

"I'll carry you," he repeated. He forced himself to move toward her and scoop her up in his arms. She felt entirely too perfect there, a sweet, warm weight that fit just right, and he wanted to hold her close and not let go.

She didn't meet his gaze while he carried her up the stairs. Both of them were silent and he wondered what she was thinking about that put that color on her cheeks, like the blush of a newly ripe apple.

"I'm the last door on the left," she whispered at the top of the stairs. The narrowness of the hallway forced him to hold her closer and he could feel each breath she took against his chest.

He opened the door she indicated and flipped on the light switch before he gingerly set her down on a wide bed covered in a rich damask.

For some reason, he would have expected her bedroom to be light and feminine. Lavender, maybe, with lace and lots of froufrou pillows. Instead, it was dramatic and bright, with strong solid colors and polished Mission furniture. She had her own small tree here in the window, as all the children did, he had noticed earlier. Her tree was decorated in framed pictures, he guessed of her children.

"Is there anything I can get you before you go to sleep? A nightgown or something?"

Her blush seemed to intensify, though he thought that might just be a reflection of the bold colors.

"I don't think so. I can hop to the bathroom and my dresser is on the way." She paused. "Um, thank you for carrying me and...everything."

"You're welcome." He gazed at her for a long moment, fighting an almost desperate hunger to touch her again. She looked so lovely, her hair tousled from sleep and that skin so rosy and soft that he ached to kiss her.

His gaze met hers and he saw a reflection of his hunger in her green eyes.

Fast on its heels was a growing unease. He could deal with all this much better if he only felt a physical attraction to her. But he was very much afraid it was becoming much, much more.

He shoved his hands in his back pockets to keep from reaching for her. "Good night, then. I'll probably sleep on the couch so I can hear if you need anything."

She opened her mouth as if to argue but shut it again, much to his relief. If he had to stay here another minute, he was going to be on that bed with her, to hell with both her broken wrist and the consequences.

"Good night, Carson. I don't know how I'll ever thank you. You've done nothing but rescue the Wheelers since you've been here."

"That's what neighbors do, right?"

With that lame comment, he backed out of the door while he still could and headed back down the stairs.

Both times he had gone up the stairs, first with Jolie then just now with Jenna, he had been too preoccupied with the Wheeler female in his arms to notice the photo gallery that lined the stairway.

But he couldn't help paying it more attention now as he moved slowly down the stairs. The pictures showed the evolution of a family. There were photographs of all of the children in various stages of development, from infants to toddlers to preschoolers on up. They were beautiful, every one of them.

He was particularly struck by the largest picture on the wall, a posed family portrait taken somewhere outdoors in the midst of what looked like golden-hued fall aspens. He stopped and gazed at it, at the trio of blond, grinning boys who looked a few years younger than they were now, and at the smiling parents behind them. Jenna looked lovely and bright and happy. Beside her stood a man who looked just like he imagined Hayden would look in twenty years or so. His face was tanned and rugged, his blond hair a shade or two darker than Jenna's. He smiled at his family like someone who knew he had everything a man could ever want.

Carson's insides wrenched with sadness for Joe Wheeler, who had been taken from his family and would never see the boys in that picture grow to manhood and who had never even met his beautiful baby girl.

He continued down the stairs, thinking of the love on those shining faces.

He was in a house full of people, but he had never been as keenly aware that he was alone.

The siren smell of coffee and something else delicious dragged her out of sleep the next morning.

Her nose twitched and as she slowly waded back to consciousness, Jenna couldn't figure out why her room was so blissfully quiet. Usually, she was either awakened by her actual alarm clock or by one of her four living, breathing, bed-bouncing alarm wannabes.

What were they up to? Maybe they had decided to let her sleep in a little. Heavenly thought, that. She opened one eye and peeked at her alarm clock, then sat upright, pushing aside the last cobwebs in a burst of panic. Eight-thirty! She never slept until eight-thirty!

She slid off the bed to her feet and then gasped when pain

shot through her left leg, at the same time she became aware of a steady, insistent throbbing in her arm.

Oh. Right. Memories flowed back of tumbling down the back stairs at Raven's Nest the previous morning, of looking at those queasiness-inducing X-rays in Jake Dalton's office, of Carson driving her home and fixing mac and cheese for her kids and wrapping her last-minute presents.

He must have put the coffee on. But what about the rest of those smells that had her stomach grumbling? And the kids must be up by now, especially on Christmas Eve morning. How long had he been coping with them on his own?

She wouldn't know until she went downstairs, she thought. She hopped to her bathroom to wash up and change, fiercely wishing she could stand under a hot pulsing shower right now. She spent a frustrating ten minutes trying to pull her hair into a ponytail with only one hand before she gave up and just ended up brushing it out and holding it away from her face with a red bandeau that matched her shirt.

She headed back through her bedroom and opened the door, only to be confronted with a sign on the wall opposite her room in big, bold, black lettering.

"Do not tackle the stairs," it read, with the second word underlined three times. "I will take you down."

Jenna gazed at the note as she balanced on one foot in her doorway. She supposed she could call down to him, but then she remembered those moments in his strong arms, how she had fought the urge the entire way up the stairs to nestle into that hard chest, to throw her arms around his neck and hold tight.

She felt entirely too delicate, too cherished, in his arms and she didn't want to become accustomed to the sensation, not when he would be returning to California and real life anytime now.

She carefully scooted down the stairs then hopped into the kitchen. The closer she went to the home's center, the more her mouth watered from the smells emanating from it.

She paused in the doorway, astonished at the sight of all her children sitting at the table while Carson stood at the microwave, removing a dish from it.

"Wow. What's all this?"

Carson looked up and his handsome features twisted into a glare. "What are you doing down the stairs? Didn't you read the sign?"

"I did. It just smelled too delicious down here, I had to follow my nose."

"Mom, Santa Claus is coming *tonight!*" Kip gushed, his features glowing like a hundred Christmas trees.

"Santa!" Jolie exclaimed, and banged her spoon on the tray of her high chair.

Her little girl was even dressed, in a holiday sweater and jeans. Warmth soaked her when she realized Carson must have found her clothes, changed her out of her pajamas and her wet diaper, then brought her down here for breakfast.

She gazed at him, looking strong and masculine in this kitchen full of children, and her heart did a long, slow roll in her chest.

Oh, she was in deep, deep trouble with him.

"I know." Jenna smiled at all her children. "Can you believe it's really here?"

They all grinned back at her, even Hayden. For the first time, she had a look at their plates and was astonished at what she saw—muffins and ham and some egg concoction that looked vaguely familiar.

"How did you do all this?" she asked Carson. "I thought you didn't cook."

"I don't. But I'm pretty mean with a microwave. When I was trying to figure out what to fix for breakfast this morning, I remembered all that delicious leftover food at Raven's Nest from the Hertzogs visit, so the kids and I made a quick trip up the hill to raid the refrigerator and freezer."

She had slept through it all? She couldn't quite take it in.

"Did you know Carson has a swimming pool and a hot tub right *inside* his house?" Hayden said.

"I did know that. I saw it when I was cooking for him and his guests."

"He says we can use it anytime we want," Drew said. "Even today. Can we, Mom?"

She had a vivid memory of the day not even a week ago when he had all but ordered her to keep her children off his property. And now he was inviting them to use his pool whenever they wanted? She couldn't quite adjust to the shift.

"That's very kind of Mr. McRaven."

"So can we go?" Kip added his voice to the chorus.

She thought of all the things she had planned for Christmas Eve. Swimming at Raven's Nest wasn't even close to showing up on the list. On the other hand, they seemed almost as excited about the idea as they did about Christmas morning.

"We'll have to see," she said. "We've got to run to Idaho Falls to pick up Grandma today, remember?"

And she had to figure out how to pare down the Christmas feast she had planned to something more manageable for someone with a bum arm and a dicey ankle.

"Have you fed the animals?" she asked.

"Not yet," Hayden said. "We were gonna do that after breakfast."

"And speaking of which, here's yours," Carson said, setting a plate down in front of her with a dramatic flourish that made Drew and Kip giggle.

The boys finished eating just a few moments later and scraped their chairs back. "If we hurry and feed the animals, we'll have more time to swim before we pick up Grandma," Drew said.

Jenna decided not to point out she hadn't yet agreed to the swim idea, though she could already see she would come across as a major grump if she said no for the sole reason that it hadn't been in her plan.

The boys hurried into the mudroom to find their coveralls and boots, leaving her alone with Carson—except for Jolie, who jabbered away in her made-up language.

"Thanks so much for breakfast," she said to Carson.

"That's my line, isn't it? You're the one who fixed it in the first place. I only nuked it."

They lapsed into silence and she was uncomfortable at the realization that her debt to him was growing by the minute.

"Carson, you don't have to stay here today. We can handle things. I'm not disoriented from the concussion anymore. I know this isn't the way you planned to spend your holidays."

"I couldn't have dreamed this scenario up in a million years," he acknowledged. "But it's not bad, either."

She could see no equivocation in his expression and realized he was sincere.

"Well, the other factor is my mother-in-law. You might change your mind about sticking around."

"Ah. The infamous Pat."

She gave a heavy sigh. "She stays here every year, Carson. She has since Joe and I married and moved here. Even after she moved to an apartment in town, she always came back for the holidays. This was her home for thirty years. No matter how wonderful her assisted-living center in Idaho Falls might be, I just can't leave her there by herself during the holidays."

He studied her, then nodded. "Of course you can't. So we'll go get her."

She expected an argument from him about how she didn't need a houseguest when she was injured. His abrupt acceptance left her a bit disoriented. "Just like that? You have no idea what she's like."

"You're her family and she's part of yours. If you want her here, we'll go get her. Are you up for a car ride to Idaho Falls? Even if I have the kids there, I'm not sure I can convince her to come with me if you're not with us."

She smiled suddenly and she would have kissed him if she could have reached him across the table.

"You're a remarkable man, Carson McRaven. You hide that soft heart very well from the rest of the world."

He looked astonished at her words and opened his mouth to argue but the phone rang before he could.

"That's probably Dr. Dalton," Carson said. "He called to check on you earlier. When I said you were still sleeping, he said he would call back to set up a time when he could stop by to see how you were doing."

She had almost forgotten her injuries, the whole reason Carson was there in the first place.

"I guess that's something else we'll have to fit in today," she said as she took the phone from him.

She couldn't help thinking how quickly and naturally they had slipped into a "we." She needed to remind herself all day that Carson's stay was only temporary.

No matter how much she was beginning to worry she wanted it to be otherwise.

"The swim was a brilliant idea," Jenna said four hours later as Carson drove the Raven's Nest's Suburban on the winding ranch road between Pine Gulch and Idaho Falls.

"I have my moments." He smiled at her and Jenna had to fight hard not to let it slip inside her heart. She would see if he still felt like grinning an hour from now after they picked up her mother-in-law.

The calm car ride was such an anomaly that she had to look in the backseat again to make sure the boys hadn't jumped out a few stoplights ago. They weren't sleeping but they all seemed relaxed, content to just look out the window or, in Drew's case, to read a book.

That they weren't bouncing off the interior walls of the Suburban was a minor miracle. Who knew a two-hour swim in Carson's pool would turn them so mellow?

Jolie had fallen asleep in her car seat before they even drove onto Cold Creek Canyon Road and Jenna was feeling comfortable herself, with jazz Christmas carols playing on the stereo and the heater sending out comforting warmth while the wipers beat back a light snowfall.

She fought sleep for a few more miles and jerked herself upright when she found herself dozing off.

"Go to sleep," Carson said. "I'll wake you up when we hit Idaho Falls so you can direct me to your mother-in-law's place."

True to his word, Carson nudged her awake a short time later and she gave him the address. After they pulled up to the elegant facility, they went inside to find Pat waiting on one of the chairs in the lobby of the assisted-living center with her walker and her small suitcase beside her.

"I thought you said two-thirty," she said without preamble. Pat's speech was only slightly slurred, though the left side of her face had been permanently paralyzed from the stroke's after-effects.

Jenna glanced at the clock above the office desk that said 2:45. "Sorry we're a little late. Merry Christmas, Mom." She limped forward carefully and kissed Pat's wrinkled cheek.

Pat gazed at her cast and the cane she was using to stabilize herself. "What happened to you?"

"I had a little accident yesterday and slipped on some ice."

"Didn't your boys shovel the walk?" she asked, her tone accusatory.

Jenna was spared from having to tell her where the accident occurred by the boys' impatience to greet their grandmother.

They all hugged her and Pat's stern expression softened at the unfeigned affection from her grandchildren.

Suddenly her gaze landed on Carson, who had carried Jolie inside. "Who are you?" she asked abruptly.

His gaze met Jenna's, a clear question in them. He was asking if he should lie about his identity to make the holiday run more smoothly for her, she realized. She was touched by the thought and even briefly entertained it, then discarded it. Beyond the fact that she couldn't let her children see her trying to carry off a lie, it wouldn't be fair to Carson to make him a party to that kind of deception.

"Mom, this is Carson McRaven. Our neighbor."

Even though half of her face remained stoic and expressionless, the other half clearly showed her outrage. "What is *he* doing here?"

Jenna braced herself, hoping Pat didn't cause a scene in front of the children. "He has been so wonderful to help us since my accident. We would have been lost without him."

"Carson has a pool inside his house, Grandma," Kip said cheerfully. He slipped his hand inside his grandmother's curled-up left one. He was always grateful to have new ears, and besides that, Pat had always adored his chatter. "We went swimming there today and played water basketball and everything. I didn't even have to hold on to the side the whole time. You should have seen me, Grandma."

She looked torn for a moment, as if she wanted to continue expressing her outrage, but the other boys stepped in to talk to her and she let herself be distracted.

Jenna was quite certain she had never been so grateful for the shortened attention span that was another outcome of the stroke.

She just had to hope they could keep her distracted the rest of the evening from remembering just how much she despised Carson.

Chapter Fifteen

He had never imagined he would ever come so close to decking an old lady—especially a feeble, brain-injured one.

Two hours later, Carson sat at the kitchen table in Jenna's kitchen listening to her mother-in-law's scorching comments to Jenna about everything under the sun. Why were they having soup instead of the roast beef she had been expecting? Why were the rolls store-bought instead of Jenna's famous flaky crescent rolls? Why was the cheesecake leftover pumpkin swirl instead of the raspberry Jenna knew she favored?

He had expected her nastiness to be aimed at him, and Pat hadn't disappointed. He could handle her insults about his having more money than taste and how he was wasting his time with his eco-friendly ranching ideas. But when she started to turn her scathing comments in Jenna's direction, his blood started a long, slow simmer.

He was going to have to say something. Jenna certainly was making no move to defend herself, even after Pat started in on how Kip needed a haircut and Hayden's sweater had a small hole in it and didn't Jenna know how to wash wool, after all these years?

Jenna was unfailingly sweet. She just smiled at her mother-in-law or pretended not to hear the most scathing of her comments.

"You don't really think that hairstyle is attractive, do you?" Pat said out of nowhere. "You look like you just climbed out of bed."

That's it. He couldn't take anymore. He opened his mouth to tell the old bat her daughter-in-law was just about the most gorgeous female he had ever met, but Jenna caught his gaze and shook her head vigorously.

To his shock, she limped to the seat at the table where her mother-in-law sat, leaned down and wrapped her uninjured arm around Pat, hugging her close.

"Mom, I have to tell you how glad I am you could come out to the house with us for Christmas Eve. Remember how awful last Christmas was in the hospital? Isn't it wonderful to be at The Wagon Wheel again, with family around?"

That seemed to stymie Pat. She opened her mouth then closed it again and let her grandchildren's chatter fill the space where her nasty comments had been.

"I think everything's ready. Pat, can you get the children settled in the dining room?"

The older woman nodded and took to the challenge willingly, making Carson wonder if perhaps she lashed out because of her own frustration in her limitations and was only looking for something to do with herself.

Still, he wasn't inclined to quickly forgive her, not when he had seen the hurt Jenna had tried to hide at the woman's comments.

"I'm so sorry." Jenna turned to him when they were alone in the kitchen. "She seems to be having a particularly bad evening and you're bearing the brunt of it. You don't have to stay and put up with her abuse."

He stopped her by pressing a finger to her mouth. She gazed at him, her green eyes huge, and he quickly dropped his hand but not before taking a guilty pleasure at the warmth and softness of her mouth against his skin.

"She's hitting at you even harder. Why do you put up with her?"

Jenna glanced into the other room to make sure everyone was out of earshot. "She wasn't like this a year ago, I promise you that." She spoke in a low, distressed voice and he had to fight to keep from taking her in his arms. "I wish you could have known her before the stroke. She was sweet and funny. I just keep reminding myself of the woman she used to be.

He had never known anyone like Jenna, who loved so unconditionally and could grit her teeth and smile in the midst of completely unwarranted harsh criticism.

"I promise, she's also not like this all the time. It seems to me the really terrible days are followed by several days when things feel like they're back to normal. I'm keeping my fingers crossed for tomorrow."

She was the eternal optimist. He smiled, unable to help himself from leaning forward and kissing her forehead.

She blinked up at him, clearly as startled by the spontaneous gesture as he had been, but Hayden came into the kitchen and she backed away from him, her cheeks rosy from more than the heat in the kitchen.

To his relief, Pat stayed largely silent as they ate in the dining room, where the boys had set a festive table with a red checkered tablecloth and even Christmas bowls with entwined holly leaves around the edges.

Each of the three kinds of soup were divine and he would never have known it came from her freezer if he hadn't helped her thaw it and stick it in Crock-Pots before they left for Idaho Falls.

After dinner, all of them helped with cleanup then they adjourned to the living room, where her busy, slightly lopsided tree gleamed against the windows.

He stoked up the fire while Pat took the easy chair and Hayden and Drew set up a card table.

The evening passed with astonishing speed as they sang Christmas carols and ate popcorn and played games of cards and Christmas charades.

"All right, that's the last game," Jenna finally said. Jolie had again begun to droop and even Kip had hidden a yawn or two behind his hand.

"There are four presents under the tree in green paper with gold bows. Hayden, can you find them and pass them out?"

"Present!" Jolie summoned enough energy to clap her hands.

"Can we open them?" Kip asked.

"Yes. Only this one, though. The rest have to wait until tomorrow."

Kip and Drew buzzed with anticipation, though Hayden looked bored with the whole thing.

"You're not excited?" Carson asked him in a man-to-man kind of tone.

He shrugged. "It's just pajamas. She makes us some every year. Big deal."

Big deal? Carson looked at the pajamas the other boys were pulling from the paper. They were flannel in complementary plaids and looked just like store-bought pajamas, from what he could tell.

"Your mother made those? As in taking material and thread and cutting out patterns and sewing them?"

"Well, yeah. What did you think I meant?"

He was utterly flabbergasted as he imagined her finding time in her chaotic life to sew four sets of pajamas. His own mother couldn't even be bothered to go to the Salvation Army to buy him a used Matchbox car but Jenna had painstakingly sewn her four children pajamas.

"Go shower and change into them and come down so I can get a picture. Then we can read," she said while he was still reeling from the contrast.

"Do you need me to give Jolie her bath?" he asked.

"I think I'll forgo it and give her one tomorrow. She's so tired she's going to be asleep in a minute as it is."

He nodded and helped change her and dress her in the little red plaid nightgown her grandmother had helped her open.

"I can't believe you made pajamas," he said as he pulled the nightgown over Jolie's curls.

Jenna shrugged. "It's not really hard. Well, the first time was, but I've been making them from the same pattern now for years, except for Jolie's nightgown, of course. I've kind of gotten into a routine."

She was a wonderful mother. He wanted to tell her so but the words seemed to catch in his throat and he turned his attention back to her daughter.

She took several digital photos of them in various poses by the Christmas tree alone and with their grandmother. He insisted on taking his turn behind the camera so she could be included in the picture as well. That offer earned him a grateful smile, then Jenna pulled out their Christmas book Advent basket.

There were still a couple of other wrapped books left but she focused on a small one that had "Christmas Eve" written on it, as well as Hayden's name.

"Why does it have my name on it?" the boy asked. "It's not my turn. I picked one two nights ago, remember?"

"Open it," Jenna answered with a soft smile.

He looked baffled as he ripped the paper away, then he stared for a long moment at the small black book in his hands.

"It's Dad's Bible." His voice was hushed as he traced his fingers over the embossed gold letters. He looked close to tears and Carson felt a lump rise in his own throat.

"We gave him that when he turned twelve years old," Pat spoke from the corner, her voice more gentle than Carson had heard.

Jenna's eyes were moist as well and she pressed her cheek on Jolie's curls. "You're ten now. Almost as old as he was when he got it. I think he would have wanted you to have it now."

Hayden dashed a surreptitious hand against his eyes and straightened his shoulders inside the flannel pajamas his mother had sewn for him.

"Do you want to read the story?" she asked.

"Really? You want me to?"

"Go ahead. Luke Chapter 2."

He turned the pages as if they were made of spun gold and finally found the right section.

"'And it came to pass in those days, that a decree went out from Caesar Augustus…'" he began, his voice solemn.

They all sat spellbound, even Drew and the energetic Kip.

Carson had never heard anything as sweetly powerful as this child's faltering voice reading the story of the first Christmas from his deceased father's Bible. He had to swallow hard several times as emotions seemed to well up inside him.

By the time the boy read the last word, Carson, who had always considered himself a skeptic, was almost ready to believe in miracles.

He hadn't dared look at Jenna while Hayden read. Still, when the boy finished, he shifted his gaze and found her wiping away tears. But she gave a watery smile and pulled Hayden close.

"Perfect. Thank you, Hayden. Your dad would have been so proud of you."

He held the Bible to his chest. "Can I keep it in my room?"

"Yes. I know you'll be careful with it so your brothers can have their turn to read the story from it in the coming years. All right, everyone. It's time for bed."

He might have expected arguments from the boys—it *was* Christmas Eve, after all—but they were subdued as they headed for the stairs.

"I'm off to bed, too," Pat said.

Jenna looked at her with surprise. "Are you sure, Mom?"

"I'm tired," the other woman said, somewhat waspishly. "Been a long day."

"Of course. Do you need help?"

"Just take care of the kids," Pat said.

"All right. Merry Christmas, Mom."

The woman nodded abruptly then shuffled out of the room with her walker.

"I'll take Jolie," he said to Jenna when Pat left. She held the girl out and he scooped her into his arms. She wasn't asleep but she was almost there. Still, she gave him a wide, sleepy smile then rested her cheek against his chest. He pressed a hand on her little back, not at all sure what to do with this wild rush of emotions churning through him.

Jenna hopped up the stairs, putting minimal weight on her ankle. He was loathe to relinquish Jolie so he followed Jenna, the little girl in his arms, as she moved from bedroom to bedroom saying prayers with her boys and giving kisses.

Finally it was Jolie's turn and he carried her to her pretty pink bedroom. He set the girl in her crib and Jenna came forward to settle her in. He started to slip out of the bedroom but Jolie held her arms out.

"Mister, kiss!"

He froze at the door then returned to the crib and leaned down. Jolie threw her tiny arms around his neck and planted a big sloppy kiss on his cheek.

She might as well have carved out his heart and tucked it under her pillow.

"Night night," she said.

"Good night," he answered, his voice gruff.

Jenna smiled at him as if she knew just what he was going through. She kissed her daughter as well, turned on a low music box by the crib, then turned the light out.

She started to hop down the stairs. Carson looked at her for a half second, heaved a long, frustrated sigh and scooped her up as he had Jolie, trying not to notice all over again how perfectly she fit into his arms.

He made it down the stairs in record time and quickly set her down on the couch in the living room.

"Now what?" he asked, his voice abrupt, mostly because it was taking all his energy and attention to keep his hands off of her.

She smiled, though he thought it looked a little strained. "Now we wait."

"For?"

"For them all to fall asleep, which on Christmas Eve can take forever. But they know Santa can't come until they're down."

She paused and studied him. "Would you like some hot cocoa while we wait?"

He wasn't a big cocoa drinker. On the other hand, having a mug in his hands might help him keep them to himself.

"I'm just going to check on Pat first before I make the cocoa."

"Can I do anything?"

"Just relax."

He nodded and leaned his head against the back of the couch. He had never realized how exhausting the whole family thing could be. He'd been up since before seven when he heard the first stirring from upstairs, and he hadn't slept that great on the narrow sofa to begin with.

He watched the Christmas tree's reflection in the window while soft instrumental carols emanated from speakers in the corners and wondered what the hell was happening to him.

He must have dozed off for a moment, though not for long. He woke to the smell of chocolate and the vanilla and cinnamon scent of Jenna.

She stood in the doorway watching him, a funny expression on her face.

"Sorry. I didn't mean to wake you," she murmured. "You can go back to sleep."

"No. I'm up." He straightened, wondering how long she had watched him. "How's Pat?"

"Fine. She was nearly asleep when I checked on her. I sometimes forget how exhausting the children can be for someone who's not used to it."

He didn't like thinking he might have the same degree of fortitude as a seventy-year-old stroke victim.

"Sit down. Get off your ankle," he ordered.

She complied with such docile alacrity, he knew she must be hurting. "I left the cocoa in the other room. I was afraid of dumping it all over the carpet if I tried to carry it."

"I'll grab it."

He found the mugs by the stove and had to smile. In typical Jenna style, this wasn't ordinary hot cocoa out of a packet. It was thick and rich and topped with whipped cream and crushed red-and-white peppermint candies.

He shook his head and carried them both to the living room. Jenna had stretched her foot out on the recliner and he set the cocoa on the small table beside her.

"Thanks."

This was nice, he thought. Just the two of them and the crackling fire and the Christmas tree. It was too nice. He could feel himself start to weave all kinds of scenarios that mostly involved sweeping her off that chair and into his lap.

"Tell me about what Christmases were like when you were a kid," he said.

She looked startled but then began telling him about her childhood, about her parents who had spoiled both her and her brother every Christmas, about big, noisy parties with her extended family.

He listened, sometimes interjecting a skillfully crafted question that would keep her going so she wouldn't ask him about his own Christmas memories.

Some time later, she lapsed into silence. "I'm worse than Kip. I'm sorry. I didn't mean to talk your ear off."

"I didn't mind," he answered, and it was the honest truth. He loved listening to her stories. She could have been reading a cookbook and he probably would have sat here just as spellbound.

She gazed at him and something changed in her eyes, a soft

light that stole his breath. Currents zinged between them and he could feel the inexorable tug of desire stretch and pull between them. His blood turned sluggish and he could hear his pulse in his ears.

Jenna jerked her gaze away and focused on the Christmas tree. "I think they're probably asleep by now. It's been an hour."

Had that much time really passed so quickly? He couldn't quite believe it.

"I had better check to make sure they're down," she said, and started limping for the stairs.

Stubborn woman. "I'll do it. Stay here."

He headed back up the stairs and moved from room to room, looking for any sign of activity. Everyone's eyes were closed, their breathing even. There was always the chance somebody could be faking but he didn't think so. He spent an extra long time in Kip and Drew's room, trying to gauge whether Drew might have quickly hid a book under his blanket when he heard footsteps on the stairs, but he couldn't see anything.

"All snug in their beds," he told Jenna when he returned downstairs.

"Now the fun begins. I'm afraid you're going to have to do most of the work."

She sent him down to the basement several times to bring up all the gifts from her various hiding places, including the gifts he had wrapped the night before.

She sat on the floor by the tree, arranging them all underneath, then filled and hung stockings. The air was filled with the scent of the apple wood fire, with cinnamon from the ornaments, with the sharp, tangy smell of the tree.

"I think that's everything," she said some time later, giving careful scrutiny to the room. "It looks just right, doesn't it?"

"I can't imagine any four children will have a better Christmas," he told her with complete sincerity.

Her smile seemed to light up the dark night. After a moment, it slid away but she continued to look at him.

"I have to tell you something," she said.

He said nothing, waiting for her to continue.

After a long moment, she sighed, fretting with the edge of her festive red cast. "I've been dreading tonight for weeks. Well, this part of it, anyway."

He blinked, astonished. She was all over the whole Christmas thing. Everywhere he looked, he saw signs that she had been planning this night for a long time.

"You've been dreading it?"

"Don't get me wrong. I can't wait for the morning. But I didn't really want to be alone after the children were in bed for the Santa Claus part. It helped so much to have you here."

Her smile wavered a little but she straightened it again. "And not just because of the heavy lifting, though I was glad for that, too."

He ached inside for all she had lost and for the courage it must take her to reshape her family's traditions without her husband.

"Thank you for letting me be part of it," he answered.

She said nothing for a moment, then before he quite realized what she intended, she stepped forward and kissed him.

Her mouth was soft and tasted of cocoa and peppermint candies, a delicious combination. He recognized the kiss for what it was, quiet gratitude, and he forced himself to remain still as her mouth moved gently against his.

Emotions swirled around them, wrapping them in the quiet peace of the night, and he wanted this slow kiss to go on forever.

Finally she eased away with a tremulous smile, her green eyes catching the lights flickering in the tree, and he was staggered by her loveliness.

"Good night, Carson. Merry Christmas."

"Can you make it up the stairs?" His voice came out gruff.

She nodded and made her way to the bottom of the staircase. She looked at him for a long, drawn-out moment, then gripped the rail and hobbled up the steps.

He sat in the living room for a long time after she disappeared upstairs, watching the fire and the tree lights reflected in the window.

He would have to leave the Wheeler house soon. Too many of the protective walls around his heart were tumbling down. He needed time and distance to shore them back up again.

No matter how high the cost.

"Mom! Is it morning? Can we go down yet?"

Jenna groaned and rolled over. In the glow of the hall light, she saw all four of her children—even Jolie, though she looked half-asleep in Hayden's arms. Jenna was quite certain her brothers had awakened her and dragged her out of bed so they could present a united front.

She looked out the window of her bedroom, where dawn hadn't even started to dress in her pearly gray colors.

"It's barely six a.m. Are you sure you don't want to sleep a little longer?"

"No!" Kip said loudly. "Santa came. I know he did. Can we go down? Please, Mom?"

She supposed she should be grateful they honored the strict family rule that no one was to go downstairs until they all went down, and that was only after she had a chance to light the fire and turn on the Christmas lights first.

She briefly toyed with trying to get them to go back to sleep, but she realized how futile that would be. "All right. Everybody hop in my bed to stay warm while I go down to make sure everything's ready."

She quickly brushed her teeth, washed her face and pulled her hair back into a ponytail, grateful all over again that she had showered last night after Jake Dalton had given her permission, as long as she covered her cast with plastic.

As she gingerly made her way into the hallway, she smelled coffee brewing. Downstairs, she discovered Carson wasn't on the living room sofa and the blankets and pillows he had used were folded up on the edge.

The fire was merrily crackling away and every light on the tree blazed a welcome.

Had he left? she wondered, and was astonished at how bereft the thought left her. But then she heard a low murmur of voices in the kitchen and her mood instantly lifted.

She followed the sound, grateful her ankle wasn't protesting too strenuously when she put weight on it.

In the doorway, she paused, completely astonished at the sight of Pat and Carson sitting at the kitchen table, coffee mugs between them, looking like old friends.

"Morning," Pat said with her half smile.

Jenna blinked. "Hi."

"Your mother-in-law and I were just talking about some of our newfangled methods at the ranch. I'm going to give her a tour of the accelerated grazing rotation one of these days. In return, she's going to tell me how she and her husband ever got anything to grow on that hundred-acre parcel above the fire road."

Jenna wouldn't have been more startled if the two of them had been in here line dancing to "Grandma Got Run Over by a Reindeer."

"Um, okay," she finally managed to say. "Well, the kids are awake and are dying to come down. I'm afraid they're going to break down my bedroom door any minute now."

Pat chuckled, a rusty sound in the quiet kitchen. "Our Joe was always the same way. He couldn't stand waiting until his dad set up the old movie camera with the six-bulb flash that just about blinded us every Christmas."

Jenna touched her mother-in-law's shoulder and Pat reached a hand up to cover her fingers.

It would be a good day today, she hoped.

They adjourned to the living room, where Jenna gave Carson the video camera duties. With her broken wrist and Pat's trembling, she figured he would get the best images.

"Mom, can we come down *yet?*" Drew called from upstairs. She shared a smile with the other two adults.

"You had better," she answered, "or Santa might decide to come and take all this stuff back to the North Pole with him."

With shrieks of excitement, the boys stampeded down the stairs and the fun began.

Chapter Sixteen

Christmas morning at the Wheeler house was an unforgettable experience.

It was impossible not to be caught up in the children's wonder and glee as they opened their presents and exclaimed over each one, from the Lifesaver book in their stockings to the iPod Hayden apparently had placed at the top of his list.

The children gave Jenna small gifts they had made in school and a new sweater and earrings they confessed their Aunt Terri had helped them pick out. They also had gifts for their grandmother, small knickknacks from the dollar store and framed pictures they had painted to decorate her small set of rooms at the assisted-living center.

To his astonishment, Drew—who had co-opted gift delivery to each recipient—handed Carson a small pile of presents.

"They're from us," Hayden said, when Carson continued to stare at the gifts.

"You didn't have to do that."

"We wanted to," Jenna assured him. "The children and I wanted to thank you for helping us so much these last few days."

They all smiled at him and he swallowed hard and turned to the presents. There were three, each rather clumsily wrapped. Jenna couldn't have done it with her broken wrist so he guessed the boys had pitched in.

The first one he picked up was heavy. He weighed it in his hands and frowned, trying to figure out what it might be. "Is it a rock?" he asked.

Kip giggled. "Open it! Open it!"

He peeled the paper away carefully, aware of an odd need to savor the moment. He opened the plain brown cardboard box and started to laugh. "It *is* a rock!"

"It's a fossil," Drew informed him. "We looked it up after we found it and it's a trilobite. Cool, huh?"

"We thought maybe you could use it as a paperweight, if you want to," Hayden said.

"We found it in the arroyo above the creek bed at the ranch a few summers ago," Jenna added. "There's a really great spot for fossils there."

"We can show you sometime if you want," Drew said.

He forced a smile, immeasurably touched. "That would be great."

"Mister, present!" Jolie pointed to the other two on his lap. The next one was cylindrical and light and he decided not to try to guess.

It was a soup-size can, he saw when he tore the paper, covered in masking-tape pieces and some sort of brown polish that made it look like leather.

"When did you have time to do all this?" he asked Jenna with some astonishment.

"When you went back to Raven's Nest for an hour or so to check in with Neil Parker yesterday when Dr. Dalton was here, remember? We made it then."

He cleared his throat, astounded at the thick emotion welling up inside him for a humble little pencil holder.

The third one was the most unexpected of all. It was the size of a deck of cards and about the same shape. When he tore the paper, he found a slim white box. Inside nestled on a small piece of cotton batting was a bolo tie with a black leather string and a smooth, flat iridescent green stone in the middle.

"It was one of my dad's," Hayden said. "He had a lot. He collected 'em and this one was broken, see, the front fell off. My mom was gonna throw it away but when we were looking for gifts for you yesterday, she remembered it so we fixed it with a polished rock."

"The stone is jasper and it came from the ranch," Jenna told him. "We found it several years ago on the hillside right about where you built your house. I always thought it was so pretty. The boys and I polished it along with some others a few years ago and I've kept it in my jewelry box, hoping I could find something to do with it someday. It fits perfectly on the tie, don't you think?"

He couldn't speak as emotions crowded through him, fast and fierce, so thick he could barely breathe around them.

He looked at Jenna, so lovely and bright, and her children, all watching him out of smiling green eyes that matched the stone on the tie, and his throat seemed to clog up. To his horror, he felt tears burn behind his eyes.

He felt as if all the careful protections he had erected around his heart had just melted to nothing like a snow fort under a blazing summer sun.

In the midst of their chaotic Christmas preparations—and Jenna dealing with a broken wrist and sprained ankle—they had taken time to make him such precious gifts.

He couldn't comprehend it. He gazed at them all and memories crowded through his head. Of Jolie falling asleep in his arms, of Kip telling him knock-knock jokes and laughing so hard at his own punch lines that Carson couldn't understand his words, of Drew swimming like a smart little fish in his pool.

Of Hayden standing a little taller and straightening his shoulders in his plaid pajamas as he read the sweet and joyful Christmas story from the Bible that had been his father's.

He loved them. All of them.

Especially their mother. She had kissed him and laughed with him and shared secrets and he had fallen head over heels with her gentleness and her sweetness and the nurturing care she showed to everyone, even when she was injured and needed it herself.

His gaze met Jenna's. Her smile had slid away and she watched him out of careful, wary eyes. He couldn't bring himself to reassure her, to smile and pretend everything was all right.

It wasn't. He loved her and he wanted her—wanted this—so much it was a physical ache in his chest.

He let out a breath. How the hell had he let this happen in just a few short days? He had spent his entire adult life protecting himself from just this, from coming to care so much, from knowing this heavy, bitter ache in his chest, as if his heart was being flayed open and dragged behind a team of horses.

He couldn't bear it. Suddenly he felt seven years old again, living in a scary flophouse, wondering what terrible thing he had done that year that had been so unforgiveable Santa Claus didn't come yet again, even though he had prayed and prayed and tried his best to be good.

Worse even than that memory was his tenth year, the year after he had spent Christmas with his grandparents and learned how magical the holidays could be.

His mother had taken him away from that, though, and on Christmas she was too high to even remember he was there. He had warmed up the last can of soup in the house for their Christmas dinner and dripped tears into it as he ate it, even though he was ten and too old to cry, remembering the lavish feast his grandmother had made the year before.

He had a terrible fear that next Christmas and every December twenty-fifth for the rest of his life would be like his tenth, only now he would compare them all to this perfect day spent with Jenna's family.

Noisy and chaotic and wonderful.

The year he learned what it meant to be part of a family.

What it meant to love.

The years stretched out ahead of him, barren and cold, and he didn't know what the hell to do about it.

"You don't like them?" Kip's subdued voice pierced his thoughts and Carson realized he must have been staring at the gifts for a long time without saying anything.

He jerked his gaze up to find them all watching him with various expression on their faces—Jenna looked concerned and the boys' expressions were cautious and a little hurt.

He cleared his throat. He had to say something. He couldn't leave them hanging like this. "I love them. All of them. The pencil holder and paperweight are both going right on my desk at McRaven Enterprises and I'm going to wear the tie the day I return to work. Thank you all so much."

The boys seemed to accept his words and their features relaxed but Jenna continued to watch him out of eyes that had turned a dark green with concern.

He forced a smile, though he was quite certain it didn't make it as far as his eyes. But Kip complained he was starving now that they were done with presents and he wanted to eat. Jenna became distracted as the others joined the chorus and the moment passed.

He had to leave, he realized as she headed into the kitchen. Now, as soon as he could. He couldn't let this family sneak any deeper into his heart. It was already going to hurt like hell trying to go on without them all.

Early in his business career, he had learned there came a time when a man had to cut his losses and walk away while he could.

That time was now.

Something was drastically wrong with Carson. Jenna could see it in his eyes.

She had no idea why the simple gifts she and the children had managed to cobble together for him at the last minute would have merited the bleakness that had entered his expression. He had looked devastated by them and she wished she had never come up with the idea.

She fretted about it as she warmed the oven for the sweet rolls and the farmer's breakfast casserole she had thawed the night before, grateful all over again that she always kept her freezer well stocked.

She was measuring the ingredients for the maple cream frosting she smeared on her sweet rolls when she glanced up and found Carson standing in the doorway, his Stetson in his hands and his ranch jacket on.

"I have to go," he said, his voice solemn but those blue eyes deep with emotions she couldn't begin to guess at.

She frowned. "Go where?"

"I gave Bill and Melina the day off so I've got to go take care of the Raven's Nest horses."

"Oh, of course. Do you need help? I could send Hayden up with you."

"No," he said, his voice abrupt.

"Okay. Um, I was thinking of moving dinner up to two since we all got up so early. Will you be done by then?"

His gaze met hers and she thought she saw something flicker in his gaze, something almost anguished, but it was gone too quickly for her to be sure. "Probably not."

"We can push it back later. That's no problem."

She was grasping at straws, she realized, desperate to avoid accepting the inevitable, that he was leaving.

"Don't worry about me, Jen." His tone was determinedly casual, though she was almost positive it was an act. "I'll just grab a bite up at the house. You're getting around okay, aren't you? You don't really need me anymore."

Everything inside her cried out an objection to that. She *did* need him. Far more than she dared admit. "My ankle feels much better today." That, at least, was the truth. "Thank you again for helping us through the worst of it."

His hands traced the brim of his hat and he looked as if he wanted to say something but he only nodded.

Something was *definitely* wrong. She could see a distance on his features that hadn't been there that morning. What had put it there? The chaos of the morning, maybe? Or their humble, haphazard gifts?

Really, who gave the CEO of a major technology innovation firm a pencil holder made from a soup can?

Her mind replayed that stunning, tender kiss the night before and the emotions that had swirled around them, between them. Had she imagined the magic of it all?

No. That had been real enough. But Carson had made it perfectly plain that while he might be attracted to her, he didn't want everything that came with her. Wet diapers, runny noses, noisy kids, preteens with truculent attitudes.

He was saying goodbye. She didn't need him to spell it out for her to understand just what this was. He was leaving, returning to his real life, and she could do nothing about it.

"So I guess I'll see you around," he said.

"Okay." She forced a smile that felt too fake, too wide. "Merry Christmas, Carson."

Again that strange something flickered in his eyes but he only nodded. "Same to you."

Without another word, he turned and walked out the door.

Jenna waited for the door to close before she pressed a fist to the hollow ache in her stomach.

He was saying goodbye. Not just for today, she knew. He wouldn't be back. She might bump into him occasionally since he was her nearest neighbor but they would revert to a polite acquaintance again, not the closer friendship they had shared these last few days.

Friendship? That was far too mild a term. She pressed a fist to her stomach again, to the tangled knot of nerves inside her and realized exactly what had happened.

She was in love with him.

With Carson McRaven, CEO of McRaven Enterprises.

How could she have been stupid enough to let this happen?

Falling in love with Joe had seemed so natural. Inevitable, even. They had been good friends in high school but hadn't dated until the summer before her senior year of college. Almost from the first, everything had seemed just right. Everyone said they were perfect for each other and Jenna had thought so, as well.

This torrent of feelings inside her for Carson was different. This wasn't perfect. It scraped at her emotions like jagged stones dragged by a flash flood and she wanted to sit on the floor of her kitchen and weep.

Still, she knew it was love. The only surprise was that she had taken so long to recognize it. She supposed she had been headed there for days, from the moment he showed up on her doorstep looking so completely out of his depth with a crying Kip in his arms.

Oh, what a disaster. Could she see any possible outcome from it other than heartbreak? He wasn't interested in a family and that's all she was, all she cared about.

Her broken wrist ached suddenly but it was nothing compared to the ache in her chest she knew no painkiller from a bottle would ease.

It was Christmas, blast it. Blast *him*. This was a time of peace, of hope. How could she feel so very miserable?

She couldn't let herself wallow in the heartache or all the pain she knew lay ahead. It was Christmas and she had promised her children the best possible holiday.

Somehow she made it through the rest of the day. The children played with their new toys and watched a couple of DVDs and ate Christmas dinner.

The only time she came close to losing it was when Hayden asked her after breakfast when Carson would come back, since he wanted to play a new video game he'd gotten from Santa with him.

When she told the boys he had gone back to Raven's Nest,

all of them had been crushed. Jenna had quickly tried to distract them, but it hadn't been easy.

Now, Jolie was asleep and the boys were close to it, exhausted from the day and especially the excitement leading up to it. She tucked them in, hugging them all a little tighter tonight in her gratitude that at least she had this.

"Will Mr. McRaven be back, Mom?" Drew asked, a solemn expression on his features. "I really like him."

Oh, she wished she could take away every disappointment her children had to face in this world. They had all come to care for Carson and would miss him and there was nothing she could do to make it better.

She forced a smile as she brushed a lock of hair away from his forehead. She pressed her lips to the skin the hair had covered. "I'm sure we'll see him again. He lives just up the hill."

"Sometimes. Most of the time he's in California, though."

She let out a breath. "True enough. But he'll be here sometimes and we can see him then."

She kissed Kip and closed their bedroom door, wondering what would be worse—never seeing him again or occasionally catching glimpses of him from afar and knowing she could never have him?

When she returned downstairs, she discovered Pat had gone to bed, as well. They were to take her home the next morning and Jenna purposely had avoided using pain pills all day so they would be out of her system when she had to drive to Idaho Falls.

Aspirin didn't quite cut it against the pain and her wrist throbbed. She told herself that was why she felt so close to tears, but she wasn't really convinced.

Now that the children were asleep and she didn't have the benefit of the distraction they provided, all the loneliness and sorrow she had suppressed all day came rushing back.

As she picked up the last straggling bits of wrapping paper and toy packaging in the living room, her mind replayed the last few days with Carson and a hundred memories washed through her. Sharing hot cocoa with him while the rest of the house slept.

His awkward efforts to put Jolie's diaper on. Seeing him in front of the stove scrubbing off dried macaroni and cheese.

That shattering kiss they had shared the night before while the Christmas tree lights twinkled and snowflakes drifted down outside.

How was she going to get through this?

She wiped at her tears. She had to. She had children who counted on her. She couldn't just take time off to wallow in self-pity and loneliness. She gave a heavy sigh and moved to unplug the Christmas tree when she suddenly spied headlights cutting through the dark night.

She frowned, even as her heart quivered in her chest. She peered through the window. It was too dark to tell if it was his black Suburban, but she couldn't imagine anyone else who might be showing up at her house this late.

Of course, she couldn't imagine why Carson might be here, either. But she could always hope.

A moment later, she heard a knock. Her heart pounded as she looked through the peephole.

Carson stood on the other side in his Stetson and ranch coat, his arms loaded with a huge box and an almost wary expression on his ruggedly handsome features.

She jerked the door open. "Carson! What on earth?"

His gaze met hers but she couldn't read his expression. "I didn't have anything for you and your kids. Let me set this down. I've got more in the truck."

She was so gloriously happy to see him, she wanted to limp after him in the snow and throw her arms around him.

On the other hand, she feared seeing him would only make her heart hurt more when he left again.

"How did you manage all this?" she asked when he came inside again. "The stores are closed on Christmas Day. Where did you possibly find one that was open?"

She thought she saw a hint of color climb his cheeks. "San Francisco."

Her jaw dropped. "What?"

He glanced up the stairs. "I guess the kids are in bed."

"Yes. I'm sorry."

"That's okay. They can open their gifts tomorrow. Well, good night. Merry Christmas." He reached for the door handle.

"Wait!" she exclaimed. "You can't just drop all this off and then leave. Aren't you going to explain to me what's going on?"

"Nothing. I just brought you and the kids some presents. I felt bad that I didn't have anything for you today." He paused. "You might as well go ahead and open it."

"Um, okay." She didn't understand any of this. She only knew she was desperately happy to see him and right now she would do anything he asked of her if it would only make him stay a little longer.

She ripped the wrapping paper away, then stared at the box as laughter and tears both fought for control inside her.

"You bought me a steam oven!"

He shrugged, looking embarrassed. "Most women would probably bash me over the head for buying them something to go in the kitchen, but I thought you might see it a little differently."

She couldn't quite believe it. She had wanted one for so long, but it had been way out of her budget! How had he possibly known? Suddenly she remembered when she had first seen his kitchen at Raven's Nest, how she had gushed over everything in it, especially the steam oven. He had noticed such an insignificant moment and tracked one down for her.

"There's more," he said. As she watched, he dumped a bag out on the floor and her heart seemed to turn over as she saw silicone spatulas and chef's cutlery and ball-tipped whisks. There seemed to be every gourmet tool she had ever dreamed about.

She gazed at the pile and then back at him. "Tell me you were joking about San Francisco."

He looked embarrassed again. "I drove to Jackson but everything was closed and to be honest, I didn't know what kind of selection I would find there anyway. On the other hand, I have a business contact who owns a chain of gourmet cooking supply stores in California." He shrugged. "He owed me a favor so he met me at one of his stores and let me in."

"Let me get this straight. You've been to San Francisco and back today."

He seemed inordinately fascinated by the twinkling lights on the garlands going up the stairs. "It's no big deal, Jen. I just wanted to give you something meaningful. And I did promise the boys the video game prototype we were working on. I was able to run by the office and pick that up while I was there and then I found a few other little things I thought they might like."

She could see several huge boxes behind him and had to wonder what his definition of "a few other little things" might entail.

All day she had fought despair, certain that she wouldn't see him again except on a casual basis. Now here he was in her living room bearing gifts for her and her children and she couldn't quite adjust to the rapid shift.

"Why, Carson?"

"I wanted to do something for you and for the kids."

"You didn't need to fly to San Francisco and back in a day to do that."

"I know."

His sigh was heavy and he finally met her gaze and she was astonished at the emotions brimming there. "I told myself I couldn't come back. I didn't plan it. But I was up at Raven's Nest looking down at your house and the smoke was coming out of the chimney and then the boys came outside to play in their new snowsuits and I couldn't take it anymore. I had to leave, so I started driving and before I knew it I was at the airport chartering a flight."

Her heart was pounding so hard she could barely hear herself think. "Why couldn't you come back?"

"Sorry?"

"You said you told yourself you couldn't come back. Why not?"

He gazed at her for a long moment and then he looked away. "I don't belong here with you and your family, Jenna. It was just a brief interlude in both our lives and now it's over."

He was going to leave again. He was even reaching for the doorknob. As she saw things, she had two choices. She could let him go, let him return to his empty life in San Francisco, to that huge empty house on the hillside.

Or she could swallow her pride and offer one more Christmas gift to him, even if he wasn't willing to accept it.

She had no choice. Not really. She stepped forward, until they were only a few feet apart, took a deep breath and plunged forward. "It's not over for me, Carson. I'm not sure it ever will be. I won't forget you or how wonderful it was to have you here these last few days."

His eyes widened and something deep and intense flickered in his gaze. "Jenna—"

"I didn't expect to fall in love with you. I certainly didn't want to. You told me yourself you're not looking for a family. I know that. I accept it. I just…wanted you to know how much you've come to mean to me these last few days. To all of us. The children love you and…so do I."

Before she even murmured the last word, he rushed forward to close the gap between them, grasped her face in his strong, wonderful hands and kissed her so fiercely all the oxygen left her lungs in an instant.

He kissed her with an almost desperate hunger and she reveled in it. She wrapped her good arm around his waist inside his coat, savoring his heat and his strength against her and the joy and peace that soaked through her.

"It killed me to leave you," he whispered against her mouth after several breathtaking moments. "I was completely wrecked, Jenna."

She heard regret and sorrow in his voice and she kissed the corner of his mouth gently. "Why did you, then?"

"Because I'm an idiot. A stupid, terrified idiot afraid to reach for the incredible prize in front of me."

She held him closer, astonished that this could be happening. The night was magical, full of sweet, healing hope.

"I love you, Jenna. That's why I took off. I've loved one other woman in my life and I failed her. I was supposed to be able to take care of her and I couldn't. When she and Henry James died, I thought my life was over. I told myself that if I blocked out anything deep or meaningful, if I focused only on business, I could protect myself from the pain and mess of love. Things were working out just fine, I thought. But then you came along and made me realize how very alone I was."

She held him tighter, astonished and grateful that she had been so very richly blessed in her life to love two such wonderful men.

He kissed the top of her head. "You showed up with your snickerdoodles and your boys and darling little Jolie and knocked down every single one of my defenses."

She smiled against his chest, even as she fought tears of joy. "I get it now. You just love me for my snickerdoodles."

He laughed softly and it was sweetest sound she had ever heard. "And your spinach rolls. And your pumpkin cheesecake. And your crostinis. And your hot cocoa with whipped cream and peppermint candy. And your…"

She stopped his recitation with the simple act of throwing off his Stetson and kissing him again.

He settled onto the sofa and pulled her onto his lap. As the tree lights flickered beside them and the fire crackled in the grate, she remembered how she had dreamed of making the ideal Christmas for her family.

She never could have imagined she would find herself here in Carson's arms with this dazzling joy surging through her.

But now, at long last, everything was perfect.

Epilogue

Raven's Nest was in chaos.

Hayden was up in his bedroom upstairs with the door open, playing "Little Drummer Boy" at full volume on the drum set his crazy mother and stepfather bought him for his eleventh birthday a few months earlier.

Amid the "ba-rump-bump-bump-bumps," Drew was chasing Kip around the great room trying to retrieve the book of Christmas mystery stories his little brother had stolen from him. But since Kip was faster than anyone in the house—and knew it—Drew was having a tough time catching him.

Frank—the new border collie puppy the boys had conned Carson into getting that summer—chased after both boys, barking at this fun new game, which Carson supposed was at least a change from the dog yanking all the ornaments off the tree.

Jolie was hanging onto his leg and gabbing a mile a minute about her dolls and the snowman they made earlier and the kitty she wanted for Christmas. And Pat, who had come to spend

Christmas Eve with them at Raven's Nest, wanted to know what time they were eating and when she was supposed to take her medicine and how much it cost to heat this mausoleum.

It was Christmas Eve.

And Carson loved it.

He picked up Jolie in his arms and answered Pat. "The radiant-heat system saves a lot of money. I'm going to have to ask Jenna about your prescriptions and what time we're eating. Hang on, I'll be right back."

As he headed toward the door with no small degree of relief, he snagged Kip by the collar of his holiday-patterned sweater as the boy jumped over an ottoman. "Give back your brother's book," he ordered.

Kip giggled but handed the book over willingly with that gap-toothed grin that had only become wider now that he was seven.

"Sorry, Drew."

His brother made a face as he snatched the book out of Kip's hand.

"You guys need to chill out a little, okay?" Carson said, though he knew it was a losing battle. "Santa's going to take one look at this place and think only wild monkeys live here. And last I heard, he doesn't make deliveries to wild monkeys."

"Why not?" Jolie asked with a little frown on her features. "Don't monkeys get presents from Santa?"

"Only if they've been good little monkeys."

"Have I been a good little monkey?" she asked.

He smiled and kissed the top of her blond curls. "You're always a good little monkey. You're *my* good little monkey."

He was crazy about this little girl, just as he loved her three brothers, drum sets, mischief, barking dogs and all.

"Go tell Hayden to either shut his door or save the recital for after dinner, okay?" he said to Drew as he carried Jolie with him into the kitchen.

Inside, Jenna was standing at the stove stirring something in a pan. By the looks of it, she had about four cooking projects going and his heart bumped at the sight of her, all pink and tousled and warm, just as it always did.

She looked up when they entered and her smile gleamed more brilliantly than the hundreds of lights on the huge Christmas tree in the great room.

He would never get tired of that smile. After six months of marriage, he adored it more than ever.

"Mommy, I'm a good little monkey," Jolie said proudly.

Jenna looked amused. "You are indeed, sweetheart."

"Put me down, please," she directed, in her best princess-of-the-manor voice, and Carson complied. Jolie raced to the sitting area off the kitchen to play with her toys scattered there.

Carson moved behind Jenna and kissed the back of her neck. "Something smells delicious," he said, his voice low.

She leaned against him with that sexy sigh of hers that drove him crazy. "It's my sticky buns."

He breathed in the scent of her, of cinnamon and vanilla and that indefinable—but infinitely sexy—scent that was plain Jenna. "Well, I do love your sticky buns," he murmured. "But I was talking about this spot right here."

He pressed his mouth again to that warm, sweet patch of skin at the back of her neck and she shivered, as she did whenever he touched her.

Their six-month wedding anniversary was in three days and he had a hard time remembering what his life was like before the Wheelers barreled into it.

They had changed everything.

He couldn't help laughing at his own stupidity whenever he thought about how certain he had been a year ago that he had all he could ever want or need. This ranch, his varied business interests, the penthouse in San Francisco.

If he had to, he would gladly trade all of that to hang on to this life he and Jenna were building together.

He had no idea a year ago how much he would love being a stepfather. Helping with homework, fishing trips in the mountains above the ranch, long weekends in San Francisco so he could catch up on work he couldn't finish long distance from Raven's Nest.

His soul filled with a quiet contentment he never realized was missing when he was lying next to Jenna while the wind hurled snow against the windows and the fire in their bedroom fireplace burned down to cinders.

He had been given more precious gifts than he could ever have imagined.

He kissed that spot on her neck again and Jenna sighed softly. "Keep that up and you're going to make me forget all I still have to do."

"That's the idea."

She turned around, her mouth set in a mock frown. "Well, you'll have no one to blame but yourself if your Christmas Eve dinner is ruined, then."

He couldn't resist kissing away that frown, pretend though it might be. "Even if we had nothing to eat but gunky orange mac and cheese or soup out of a can, Jenna Wheeler McRaven, this would still be the happiest Christmas Eve of my life."

Her eyes softened and she gave him a vivid smile as she returned his kiss.

"Do you know what the best part is?" he asked.

She shook her head, her arms around his waist.

"I have absolutely no doubt that next year will be even better. And the year after that will be better still. And I can't even imagine how great the year after *that* will be."

She rested her head against his chest and he wanted to freeze this moment in his memory—the snow falling outside, the drums still banging away upstairs, the boys' shrieks, the puppy barking, Jolie jabbering to her toys.

The memory album in his head was bulging at the seams.

"I wouldn't be so confident about future Christmases if I were you," she said with a rueful laugh. "We're going to have teenagers by then and I'm afraid all bets are off."

He didn't care. All those years and Christmases stretched out ahead of them, shiny and bright and full of promise like the presents under their tree, and he couldn't wait to unwrap every one.

* * * * *

Here is a sneak preview of
A STONE CREEK CHRISTMAS,
the latest in Linda Lael Miller's acclaimed
McKETTRICK *series.*

A lonely horse brought vet Olivia O'Ballivan to Tanner
Quinn's farm, but it's the rancher's love that might cause
her to stay.

A STONE CREEK CHRISTMAS
Available December 2008
from Silhouette Special Edition

Tanner heard the rig roll in around sunset. Smiling, he wandered to the window. Watched as Olivia O'Ballivan climbed out of her Suburban, flung one defiant glance toward the house and started for the barn, the golden retriever trotting along behind her.

Taking his coat and hat down from the peg next to the back door, he put them on and went outside. He was used to being alone, even liked it, but keeping company with Doc O'Ballivan, bristly though she sometimes was, would provide a welcome diversion.

He gave her time to reach the horse Butterpie's stall, then walked into the barn.

The golden retriever came to greet him, all wagging tail and melting brown eyes, and he bent to stroke her soft, sturdy back. "Hey, there, dog," he said.

Sure enough, Olivia was in the stall, brushing Butterpie down and talking to her in a soft, soothing voice that touched something private inside Tanner and made him want to turn on one heel and beat it back to the house.

He'd be damned if he'd do it, though.

This was *his* ranch, *his* barn. Well-intentioned as she was, *Olivia* was the trespasser here, not him.

"She's still very upset," Olivia told him, without turning to look at him or slowing down with the brush.

Shiloh, always an easy horse to get along with, stood contentedly in his own stall, munching away on the feed Tanner had given him earlier. Butterpie, he noted, hadn't touched her supper as far as he could tell.

"Do you know anything at all about horses, Mr. Quinn?" Olivia asked.

He leaned against the stall door, the way he had the day before, and grinned. He'd practically been raised on horseback; he and Tessa had grown up on their grandmother's farm in the Texas hill country, after their folks divorced and went their separate ways, both of them too busy to bother with a couple of kids. "A few things," he said. "And I mean to call you Olivia, so you might as well return the favor and address me by my first name."

He watched as she took that in, dealt with it, decided on an approach. He'd have to wait and see what that turned out to be, but he didn't mind. It was a pleasure just watching Olivia O'Ballivan grooming a horse.

"All right, *Tanner,*" she said. "This barn is a disgrace. When are you going to have the roof fixed? If it snows again, the hay will get wet and probably mold…"

He chuckled, shifted a little. He'd have a crew out there the following Monday morning to replace the roof and shore up the walls—he'd made the arrangements over a week before—but he felt no particular compunction to explain that. He was enjoying her ire too much; it made her color rise and her hair fly when she turned her head, and the faster breathing made her perfect breasts go up and down in an enticing rhythm. "What makes you so sure I'm a greenhorn?" he asked mildly, still leaning on the gate.

At last she looked straight at him, but she didn't move from Butterpie's side. "Your hat, your boots—that fancy red truck you drive. I'll bet it's customized."

Tanner grinned. Adjusted his hat. "Are you telling me real cowboys don't drive red trucks?"

"There are lots of trucks around here," she said. "Some of them are red, and some of them are new. And *all* of them are splattered with mud or manure or both."

"Maybe I ought to put in a car wash, then," he teased. "Sounds like there's a market for one. Might be a good investment."

She softened, though not significantly, and spared him a cautious half smile, full of questions she probably wouldn't ask. "There's a good car wash in Indian Rock," she informed him. "People go there. It's only forty miles."

"Oh," he said with just a hint of mockery. "*Only* forty miles. Well, then. Guess I'd better dirty up my truck if I want to be taken seriously in these here parts. Scuff up my boots a bit, too, and maybe stomp on my hat a couple of times."

Her cheeks went a fetching shade of pink. "You are twisting what I said," she told him, brushing Butterpie again, her touch gentle but sure. "I meant…"

Tanner envied that little horse. Wished he had a furry hide, so he'd need brushing, too.

"You *meant* that I'm not a real cowboy," he said. "And you could be right. I've spent a lot of time on construction sites over the last few years, or in meetings where a hat and boots wouldn't be appropriate. Instead of digging out my old gear, once I decided to take this job, I just bought new."

"I bet you don't even *have* any old gear," she challenged, but she was smiling, albeit cautiously, as though she might withdraw into a disapproving frown at any second.

He took off his hat, extended it to her. "Here," he teased. "Rub that around in the muck until it suits you."

She laughed, and the sound—well, it caused a powerful and wholly unexpected shift inside him. Scared the hell out of him and, paradoxically, made him yearn to hear it again.

* * * * *

Discover how this rugged rancher's wanderlust
is tamed in time for a merry Christmas, in
A STONE CREEK CHRISTMAS.
In stores December 2008.

Silhouette®

SPECIAL EDITION™

FROM *NEW YORK TIMES* BESTSELLING AUTHOR

LINDA LAEL MILLER

A STONE CREEK CHRISTMAS

Veterinarian Olivia O'Ballivan finds the animals in Stone Creek playing Cupid between her and Tanner Quinn. Even Tanner's daughter, Sophie, is eager to play matchmaker. With everyone conspiring against them and the holiday season fast approaching, Tanner and Olivia may just get everything they want for Christmas after all!

*Available December 2008
wherever books are sold.*

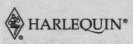

HARLEQUIN®

HOLLY JACOBS
Once Upon a Christmas

Daniel McLean is thrilled to learn he
may be the father of Michelle Hamilton's
nephew. When Daniel starts to spend
time with Brandon and help her organize
Erie Elementary's big Christmas Fair, the
three discover a paternity test won't make
them a family, but the love they discover
just might....

**Available December 2008
wherever books are sold.**

LOVE, HOME & HAPPINESS

www.eHarlequin.com   HAR75242

HARLEQUIN® *Romance*®

Marry-Me Christmas

by *USA TODAY* bestselling author

SHIRLEY JUMP

A *Bride* FOR ALL *Seasons*

Ruthless and successful journalist Flynn never mixes business with pleasure. But when he's sent to write a scathing review of Samantha's bakery, her beauty and innocence catches him off guard. Has this small-town girl unlocked the city slicker's heart?

Available December 2008.

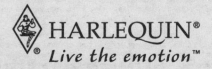

HARLEQUIN®
Live the emotion™

www.eHarlequin.com   HR17557

REQUEST YOUR FREE BOOKS!

2 FREE NOVELS PLUS 2 FREE GIFTS!

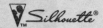 Silhouette®

SPECIAL EDITION®

Life, Love and Family!

YES! Please send me 2 FREE Silhouette Special Edition® novels and my 2 FREE gifts (gifts are worth about $10). After receiving them, if I don't wish to receive any more books, I can return the shipping statement marked "cancel." If I don't cancel, I will receive 6 brand-new novels every month and be billed just $4.24 per book in the U.S. or $4.99 per book in Canada, plus 25¢ shipping and handling per book and applicable taxes, if any*. That's a savings of at least 15% off the cover price! I understand that accepting the 2 free books and gifts places me under no obligation to buy anything. I can always return a shipment and cancel at any time. Even if I never buy another book from Silhouette, the two free books and gifts are mine to keep forever.

235 SDN EEYU   335 SDN EEY6

Name	(PLEASE PRINT)
Address	Apt. #
City	State/Prov.	Zip/Postal Code

Signature (if under 18, a parent or guardian must sign)

Mail to the Silhouette Reader Service:
IN U.S.A.: P.O. Box 1867, Buffalo, NY 14240-1867
IN CANADA: P.O. Box 609, Fort Erie, Ontario L2A 5X3

Not valid to current subscribers of Silhouette Special Edition books.

Want to try two free books from another line?
Call 1-800-873-8635 or visit www.morefreebooks.com.

* Terms and prices subject to change without notice. N.Y. residents add applicable sales tax. Canadian residents will be charged applicable provincial taxes and GST. Offer not valid in Quebec. This offer is limited to one order per household. All orders subject to approval. Credit or debit balances in a customer's account(s) may be offset by any other outstanding balance owed by or to the customer. Please allow 4 to 6 weeks for delivery. Offer available while quantities last.

Your Privacy: Silhouette is committed to protecting your privacy. Our Privacy Policy is available online at www.eHarlequin.com or upon request from the Reader Service. From time to time we make our lists of customers available to reputable third parties who may have a product or service of interest to you. If you would prefer we not share your name and address, please check here. ☐

EXTRA

THE ITALIAN'S BRIDE
Commanded—to be his wife!

Used to the finest food, clothes and women,
these immensely powerful, incredibly
good-looking and undeniably charismatic
men have only one last need: a wife!

They've chosen their bride-to-be and they'll
have her—willing or not!

Enjoy all our fantastic stories in December:

THE ITALIAN BILLIONAIRE'S
SECRET LOVE-CHILD
by CATHY WILLIAMS (Book #33)

SICILIAN MILLIONAIRE,
BOUGHT BRIDE
by CATHERINE SPENCER (Book #34)

BEDDED AND WEDDED FOR REVENGE
by MELANIE MILBURNE (Book #35)

THE ITALIAN'S UNWILLING WIFE
by KATHRYN ROSS (Book #36)

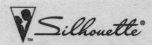

COMING NEXT MONTH

SPECIAL EDITION

Silhouette®